Mrs. Alexander

Ralph Wilton's Weird

A Novel

Mrs. Alexander

Ralph Wilton's Weird
A Novel

ISBN/EAN: 9783337031657

Printed in Europe, USA, Canada, Australia, Japan

Cover: Foto ©Andreas Hilbeck / pixelio.de

More available books at **www.hansebooks.com**

A NOVEL

BY

MRS. ALEXANDER

AUTHOR OF "THE WOOING O'T" AND "WHICH SHALL IT BE?"

NEW YORK

HENRY HOLT AND COMPANY

1875

RALPH WILTON'S WEIRD.

CHAPTER I.

THE yellow sunlight of a crisp October day was lighting up the faded though rich hangings, and the abundant but somewhat blackened gilding, of a large study or morning-room in one of the stately mansions of Mayfair, nearly fourteen years ago.

Bookcases and escritoires, writing-tables and reading-tables more or less convenient, easy-chairs, print-stands furnished with well-filled portfolios, pictures, bronzes, all the signs and tokens of wealth, were there, but nothing new. An impress of extinct vitality was stamped upon the chamber and all it contained. The very fire burned with a dull, continuous glow, neither flaming nor crackling.

On one side of this fire, his back to the light, in a high leathern chair, sat an old man. Originally slight in frame, he now looked attenuated. His blue, brass-buttoned coat, though evidently from the hands of an artist, hung loosely upon him. His thin gray hair was carelessly brushed back from a brow not high but peculiarly wide, a straight, refined nose, a square-cut chin, a thin-lipped, slightly cruel mouth, a tint of the deadliest pallor—all these combined to make his countenance at once attractive and repellent. There was a certain dignity in his attitude as he leaned against the side of the large chair, in which he was almost lost, one thin, small white hand resting on the arm of his seat, the other playing, in a manner evidently habitual, with a couple of seals hanging in by-gone fashion from a black ribbon.

He was gazing at the fire, and listening to a meek looking semi-genteel young man, who, seated at a table with a neatly folded packet of papers before him, was reading aloud from a letter. But the lecture was interrupted.

The door was thrown open by an archdeaconal butler, who announced, in a suppressed voice and impressive manner, " Colonel Wilton, my lord."

Whereupon entered a soldierly looking man, above middle height, his broad shoulders and compact waist, duly displayed by an incomparably fitting frock-coat, closely buttoned, and worn with the indescribable carriage that life-long assured position and habitual command only can bestow. A bold, sunburnt, and somewhat aquiline face, a pair of eagle-like brown eyes, and plenty of red-brown wavy hair, whisker, and

moustache, entitled the possessor to be termed by par-
tial comrades "a good-looking fellow."

The old nobleman stood up, and, raising his cold,
steely, keen blue eyes, with an extension of his thin
lips intended for a smile, held out his slight, fine
hand.

"I am glad to see Colonel Wilton," he said, in a
low, sweet voice, which must have been peculiarly
charming before age had thinned its tones.—"You
may leave us, Mr. Robbins," he added; whereupon
the young man at the writing-table took up his papers
and departed.—"I am obliged to you," continued
Lord St. George, "for obeying my summons so
promptly; it was more than I expected, considering
how often you must have been in town without calling
upon your recluse kinsman."

"My dear lord," said Colonel Wilton, with a frank
smile, taking the chair placed for him, "I never
thought a visit from me would be acceptable. I supposed that I must excite the natural aversion which
is generally felt for junior and unendowed relatives,
so I kept out of the way." Colonel Wilton's voice
was not unlike his host's, though deeper and richer.

"Unendowed or not, you are almost the only relative who has never asked me a favor," returned the
old man.

"Had I wanted anything I suppose I should have

asked for it," said Colonel Wilton, good-humoredly; " but my ambition is professional, and fortune has favored me beyond my deserts."

" You are a young colonel."

" Only brevet."

" Ay, I remember; you got your first step after that affair of the rifle-pits."

" Exactly ; then I volunteered for our second battalion when the mutiny broke out, saw a good deal of very unpleasant service, was slightly hit, got fever, more from fatigue than wounds, was ordered home on sick leave, and found my brevet awaiting me. I have just returned from the German baths—and now, my lord, I am at your service."

" You want to know why I sent for you—you shall hear presently ; " the old man paused abruptly. " You are like, and yet unlike, your father," he resumed ; " you know, I suppose, that, although but first-cousins, we might have been brothers, we hated each other so well ? "

" I have heard something of it," returned Wilton, coolly, though the smiling, frank expression passed from his face ; " but I have lived so much among strangers that I am lamentably ignorant of the family hatreds."

Lord St. George looked up, and played more rapidly with his seals. " I have been a broken man for many years," he resumed, after a short pause, "and latterly a complete recluse. Men are such knaves, and life is such a round of folly, amusement, and ambition, and 'lofty aspirations,' as modern scribblers have it, such dust and ashes, that I can with unusual truth say I am weary! I dare say you are wondering why I inflict this Jeremiad upon you—I hardly know myself; however, it is finished. I suppose you are aware that a very small portion of my property is attached to the title of St. George?"

Colonel Wilton bowed, and listened with increasing interest. "My Worzelshire estates and Welsh mines," continued the old lord, "came to me through my mother, and are to dispose of as I choose. A ruined tower and some worthless moorland is all that will come by right to you. It is in my power to make you that most wretched of failures—a poor nobleman, or to bequeath you means to ruffle it with the best."

"You must do as seems best in your eyes," said Colonel Wilton, with the same good-humored, well-bred independence which had characterized his manner all through the interview, when the peer stopped, as if for a reply.

"I am by no means inclined to separate my property from my title—but it is all in my own hands —I have no claims upon me—no nearer relative than yourself. All that I have heard of you is tolerably creditable to the family name, and I am inclined to give you the means to keep up the old title. There is one point, however, on which I should like you to understand and conform to my wishes. You are, of course, aware of the circumstance which has blighted my life—the latter half of it?"

Although it seemed impossible that any living cheek could be paler than Lord St. George's, it grew a shade more ghastly as he spoke.

" Yes, yes," returned Colonel Wilton, with a sort of quick sympathy. "Do not, if possible, distress yourself by alluding to it."

"I must, Ralph—I must!" It was the first time the viscount had called him by his name ; and he continued, in a firm but low voice: "When my daughter, my only child, flung herself into an abyss of infamy by her disgraceful marriage, I at once and forever renounced her. Now I only care that the inheritors of my name and property may at least be free from the taint of inferior race : promise me you will marry a gentlewoman, a girl of some unblemished family, which, though they are few, can still be found —promise me this, and I will leave you all I possess."

" My dear lord, it is not necessary to promise. Poor as I am, I should never dream of marrying a plebeian ; but I would rather not marry for some years to come.   I am little more than thirty; you must really leave me a longer spell of liberty."

"All young men are alike," returned Lord St. George.   "You put off the evil day until you are too old to see your children grow up, or to guide them, or be anything but a semi-living mummy, fit only to sign checks for other people to expend.   Be ruled by me ; accept my conditions, quit the army, spend the coming season among the best country-houses, pick out a suitable wife—as my heir, you *can* choose—go into Parliament, a Crimean man will be well received by country constituencies, and you will be well before the world by the time I make way for you.   I say nothing," added the old peer, with an air of courtly humility, "of the gratitude such a course would enlist from me personally.   I have no claim of that description to urge upon you."

"Your present intentions constitute a tolerable strong claim," replied Wilton, smiling.   "At any rate I should be very happy to please you, and I heartily wish you could will away your title as your estates. However, on the subject of marriage, I can make *no* promise ; at present, the mere fact of being tied seems to me to outweigh all other advantages.   I hope my bluntness does not offend you.   I should be sorry to do so.   You see, there is a strong dash of the Bohemian in my nature, though I am not without ambition, and

I am quite aware that a penniless peer is a most unfortunate devil. Still I cannot make up my mind to matrimony. Nevertheless, apart from promises, I do not think any man can be more averse to the idea of marrying out of his own class than I am."

There was a moment's pause, Lord St. George looking keenly at his companion.

"I do not think you seem likely to commit so egregious an error; but it is impossible to rely on the prudence or common sense of any man; though you are certainly past the age when men will sacrifice much for women. So I must be content with probabilities."

Another short pause, during which Colonel Wilton took up his hat, which he had laid on the carpet beside him.

"Stay," said the old peer. "It is long since I have endured to see any of my own people, and the effort cost me something. Now you are here, tell me where are your sisters, your brother?"

"My brother, poor fellow! he died of fever before he left college. My sisters are both married, the eldest to General Ogilvie—he is in command at Montreal—and Gertrude to the Dean of ——."

"I remember hearing of the first marriage," returned Lord St. George. "I was then in Greece."

He continued to ask for various persons, respecting very few of whom Colonel Wilton could give any information. Meantime the light was fading, and Lord St. George's visitor growing somewhat impatient.

"You must forgive me, my lord, if I bid you good-morning. But when I received your message I had arranged to run down to Scotland to-night for some grouse-shooting, and I am to dine early with on old brother-officer before starting."

"Then I must not detain you," replied Lord St. George, reluctantly. "I am glad I have seen you. I feel a little more satisfied about the future of my name and possessions. I wish you could meet my wishes completely. I am singularly without near relatives—singularly free from claims of any kind."

Colonel Wilton had stood up as if in the act to go ; he hesitated an instant, as his kinsman paused, and said, in a lower tone :

"I presume, then, my cousin—your daughter—left no children ? "

"Do not dare to name her, sir ! " cried the old man, fiercely, and grasping the arms of his chair with nervous, twitching fingers. "She has long ceased to live for me ! She—the first woman in a long, un-broken line—that ever brought disgrace upon her name ! Living or dead, I refuse all intelligence con-cerning her. Her children may exist, or not; the

1*

poorest beggar that crawls in the street is more to me!"

"You have, certainly. a cruel disappointment to complain of, my lord," said Wilton, gravely and firmly. "But the children would be sinless.   You would not, I am sure, leave them to suffer poverty and—"

"I would—I would! I would stamp out the spawn of such a viper! There—there, leave me.   I believe you are an honest gentleman ; but this subject you must never touch again.   Good-morning, Ralph! Let me see you on your return from the north."

Colonel Wilton promised that he would call, and pressing the thin, wan hand extended to him, left the room.

About two hours later, a couple of gentlemen sat at dinner in a private room in Morley's Hotel.   The cheese period had been reached, and the sharp edge of appetite blunted.   One, who seemed the host, was Ralph Wilton ; the guest was a tall, rugged-looking. bony man, with shaggy eye-brows and a large hooked nose, slightly bent to one side, small, sharp, dark-gray eyes, grizzled black hair, and a wide mouth, with a strong projecting under-jaw.   This does not sound like the perfection of manly beauty, yet Major Moncrief was not a bad-looking man.

" And when do you intend to join me, Moncrief?"
said Colonel Wilton.

" Not later than this day week."

" I hope not. For I have no fancy for being alone
in my glory."

The conversation flowed somewhat intermittently
until the waiter, placing wine and olives on the table,
left the friends alone.

" Help yourself," said Colonel Wilton, pushing the
claret toward Major Moncrief. " Do you know, I
have had an interview with that curious old hermit,
Lord St. George, to-day ?"

" Indeed ! How did that come about ?"

" I found a note from him at the club this morning,
inviting me, very politely, to call any day after three.
So, as I hope not to see London again for some
months, I went at once."

" You are his heir, are you not ?"

" To his barren title—yes ; but he can will away
his wealth as he likes. Poor old fellow ! He had
an only child, a lovely girl, I believe, and, after refusing
some of the best matches in England, she ran off with
an artist fellow who played the fiddle, or sang divinely,
and the viscount never forgave her. I only know the
general gossip, but I have been told she died in fright-
ful poverty. I ventured to say a word in favor of the
possible and probable children, and was soon pulled

up for my pains. How idiotic women are, and yet how keen and hard at times! This cousin of mine was not so very young either; she must have been four-and-twenty."

"Women are quite incomprehensible," ejaculated Moncrief.

Colonel Wilton laughed.

"Well, old St. George, it seems, sent for me to induce me to marry some 'Clara Vere de Vere,' in order to secure the sacred title and acres from falling into the hands of a half-breed inheritor. However, though I would not acknowledge his suzerainty by giving him the promise he wanted, he may be tolerably sure I would never marry a second-rate woman. I do not mean to say I care for rank, but good blood is essential."

"I do not fancy you are much of a marrying man."

"No! not at present. I shall come to it some day. I have been too busy to have had an attack of the love-fever for a long time."

"You were badly hit in that affair with Lady Mary," observed Moncrief.

"Well—yes! But I made a rapid recovery. Then, matrimony would be a different matter. In short, if Lord St. George will just give me a year or two more of liberty, I dare say I shall be ready to present him with a bride of the desired pattern. I really have no democratic proclivities."

"Ah ha, lad!" said Moncrief, in his unmistakable Scotch tones, "you must just 'dree your weird.'"

"So must every one," returned Wilton, rising to fill his cigar-case from a box that stood upon the sideboard. "But I think I have survived the spooney period, and have sown my wild oats—not that I have had more than a mere handful to dispose of. On the whole, I have been a pattern man—eh, old fellow?"

"Hum! There have been more extensive crops," returned the major, doubtfully. "Still, do not be too sure of yourself."

"Oh, I am safe enough. And, besides," he continued, returning to the table and filling his glass, "I am very particularly anxious that Lord St. George should leave me something wherewith to regild the faded honors of his ancient peerage. I confess to a mortal dread of being a poor peer. If my old kinsman does not leave me his property, I will never adopt the title, but be plain 'Ralph Wilton' to the end of the chapter."

"You might do worse," said Moncrief, dryly. "As I said before, you must 'dree your weird.'"

"Halloa!" cried Wilton, suddenly; "half-past seven, by Jove! I shall have a close shave to catch the train!" He rang the bell, ordered a cab; hastily donning his overcoat and thrusting his cigar-case into the breast-pocket, he shook hands heartily with his friend. "Good-by, old fellow; come as soon as you can, and let the moorland breeze sweep the cobwebs from your brain. You are too solemn by half for so good a comrade—good-by!"

It was a very close shave; but Ralph Wilton was just in time. The bell had rung before he had taken his ticket, after seeing a favorite pointer properly disposed of. "Here you are, sir," cried a porter, opening the door of a carriage. Wilton jumped in, and the door was slammed. "Stop! I say, porter," he shouted, as he glanced at the only other occupant, thinking to himself, "An unprotected female! this is too formidable!" But his voice was drowned in the loud panting of the engine, and they were off. "It cannot be helped," he thought, and set about arranging himself as comfortably as he could.

His companion was a young lady, he perceived, as his eyes became accustomed to the lamp-light. She was in black, and rather thinly clad for a night-journey. Her bonnet lay in the netting overhead. And a blue scarf was loosely tied over her head and ears. She seemed already asleep, though Wilton was dimly aware that she had opened a pair of large dark eyes to look at him. She was a serious drawback to the comfort of his journey. But for her he could make a bed of the cushions, and stretch himself at full length; but for her he could solace himself with unlimited cigars, and enjoy the freedom of loneliness. Thinking thus, he stooped forward to take up an evening paper he had snatched at the last moment, and his cigar-case fell from his pocket. His obnoxious fellow-traveller opened her eyes. " If you smoke," she said, " do not mind me; it may help me to sleep." With a slight shiver she closed her eyes again, apparently without hearing Wilton's thanks, while his unspoken male-dictions on the ill chance that placed her in the same carriage were, in some mysterious way, silenced and arrested by the charm of a soft, sweet voice, delicate yet full, with a certain sadness in its tones, and an accent not quite English. " A gentlewoman, I im-agine," thought Wilton, as he moved from his place to the centre seat opposite her to be nearer the light. There was something touching in the childlike aban-donment of her attitude; her head lay back in the angle of the division she occupied; her face was very pale, and a dark shade under the eyes bespoke fatigue. Long black lashes fringed her closed eyes, curling back at the ends, and all of color was concentrated in her delicately-curved lips. Ralph Wilton could not help glancing from his paper to her face, and forming con-jectures respecting her. Why did her people let so fair, so young a creature wander about by herself?

But he was by no means old enough to adopt a fatherly view of so pretty a subject. She must be seventeen or eighteen—here his companion murmured in her sleep, and sighed deeply ; while Wilton, with a sudden access of chivalrous modesty, reproaching himself for presuming upon her unconsciousness to scan so closely the tender, childlike face that lay hushed before him, withdrew to his original position. Here he tried to read, but the face and figure of the old recluse noble-man flitted between him and his paper, and the bitter-sweet of his tone sounded again in his ears—what depths of disappointment and mortification that old man must have fathomed ! Well, worse endings might have come about than the union of Lord St. George's title and property in his (Ralph Wilton's) favor ; and, if he ever inherited these good things, he would certainly look up his erring cousin's children. These medita-tions were varied by sundry glances at his companion, vague conjectures concerning her. How soft and gentle her mouth looked ! Yet there was a good deal of power in the wide, smooth forehead and delicately but clearly marked dark-brown eyebrows. As Wilton looked he perceived her shiver, without waking, and make a sleepy effort to fold her shawl closer. The night was growing colder, and Wilton, observing a small portion of the window next his companion open, rose to shut it. In moving to accomplish this, he touched the slumberer's foot. She opened her eyes with a sleepy, startled look—great, dark, lustrous eyes, which seemed to banish the childlike expression of her face.

"I beg your pardon," said Colonel Wilton; "but it is cold, and I thought you would like the window shut."

"Oh, yes, thank you; it is very, very cold." She sat up and rubbed her hands together, tying the blue scarf closer round her head, and thrusting carelessly under it a heavy tress of very dark-brown hair, that had become loosened, with utter disregard of appearances, as if only desirous of rest. "I am so, so weary," she went on, "and I dream instead of sleeping."

"That is probably because of your uneasy position," said Wilton. "If you will allow me to arrange the cushions for you, I think you may rest better—I am an old traveller."

"You are very good," she returned, hesitatingly; "how do you mean?"

"I will show you;" and he proceeded to make supports for one of the unoccupied cushions with a walking-stick and umbrella so as to form a couch, and then rolled up his plaid loosely for an *impromptu* pillow. "Now," he said, with frank good-nature, "you can rest really; and, if you will wrap yourself in my cloak, I dare say you will soon forget you are in a railway-carriage."

" Thank you very much," she replied. " How good of you to take so much trouble—and your plaid, too ! You have left yourself nothing ! "

" Oh, I do not need anything ! Take the cloak, and I wish you good-night."

He checked an inclination to wrap it round her, lest she might think him too officious ; and, smiling at the change in his own sentiments toward his fellow-traveller, withdrew to his original position.

" At least you can smoke," said she, as she placed herself upon the couch he had improvised. " I really like the perfume of a cigar."

Thus encouraged, Wilton drew forth his cigar-case and comforted himself with a weed, while he had the satisfaction of observing the perfect stillness of the rather shapeless mass of drapery made by his heavy cloak round the slender form slumbering beneath it. So they sped on into the night. Wilton's cigar was finished ; he threw the end from the window. Gazing a moment at the dim, uncanny trees and hedges as they flew past with ghastly rapidity, and settling himself in his corner, he too tried to sleep for a long time in vain. The past—the possible future—the absolute present—his sudden interest in his companion, crowded and jostled each other in his thoughts, but gradually all became indistinct, and at last he slept.

Uneasily, though—visions of struggles—of men and horses dying—of a desperate necessity to carry an order from the general to a remote division, and the utter impossibility of getting his horse to move—dreams like these distracted him ; at last a heavy battery on his left opened fire, and he woke.

Woke suddenly, completely, with a feeling that the end of everything was at hand. A noise of tearing and crashing filled his ears, mingled with shrieks and yells ; the carriage heaved violently, first to one side, and then to the other, in which position it remained.

As Wilton sprang to his feet, his fellow-traveller started quickly to hers ; and, grasping his arm, exclaimed, with a certain despairing calm that struck him even in such a moment: " Is it—is it death ? "

He did not reply ; but, holding on by the bar which supports the netting over the seats, he managed to open the door next him. It was on the upheaved side, and he found a heap of clay jammed under the step of the carriage.

" Come," he exclaimed, " give me your hand !— lean on my shoulder—there is an open space beyond here."

His fellow-traveller obeyed, silently and steadily.

Instinctively Wilton groped his way across what seemed a truck laden with earth and stones, and assisted his companion down the opposite side on to the grass-grown border of the line, which was open, and only fenced by a low bank and hedge. Placing her in safety, he turned to look at the scene of fear and confusion. A few yards ahead lay the massive fragments of the two engines heaped together, the foremost carriage smashed to pieces and already blazing, having caught light from the guard's lamp, which had been overturned. Two other carriages, more or less injured, were, like the one he had just quitted, forced upon trucks laden with stone and clay. The passengers were scrambling over them, the women screaming, the men shouting directions and questions.

" If you will stay here, I will go and see if I can be of any use," exclaimed Wilton. " You are quite safe, and I will return as soon as I can."

She murmured something in reply as he went forward.

CHAPTER II.

WILTON found an indescribable scene of confusion when he came up to the overturned
engine. The male passengers and some twenty nav-
vies, who had been with the ballast train, were trying
frantically to separate the burning carriages from the
others by forcing them back ; but, although the coup-
ling irons were broken, the foremost carriages had
been so violently dashed against the trucks that they
had become too closely entangled to be stirred, and
it seemed highly probable that the whole train would
be consumed before any means could be devised for
extinguishing the flames. Wilton's quick eye took in
the difficulty in a moment, and noticed that the blazing van, having been the first to encounter the shock,
had fallen on the side away from the ballast train,
breaking the couplings and everything breakable as
it crashed over. The next carriage had been forced
upon the second truck, and the others more or less
upon those nearest them, as they were farther from
the actual collision. The unhappy guard had been
dragged senseless from the *débris;* there was, there-

fore, no one to direct the willing but fruitless efforts
of the volunteers. Seeing this, Wilton sprang upon
the truck nearest him, and shouted, in clear, ringing
tones:

"Hold, men! you will never move that wreck!
Your only chance to put out the flames is to smother
it with the damp clay here. Get your shovels and
picks—some of you jump up with the picks and loosen
the stuff; another party be ready with the shovels to
pile the clay over the fire."

At the first sound of authoritative direction the
men sprang to obey, and Wilton took as supreme
command as if a party of his own pioneers were at
his orders. The men worked with a will, as men
generally do when intelligently and energetically com-
manded. It was a wild and not unpicturesque scene.
At first the flames from the dry varnished wood
streamed out upon the breeze, which, fortunately, was
not high, though it sometimes sent wreaths of smoke
and fire against the men who were toiling to extin-
guish it, and bringing out in strong relief the figure of
Wilton, who had climbed upon the side of the carriage nearest the burning fragments, and, holding on
with one hand, urged the working party with quick,
commanding gestures. By the time the truck had
been half emptied the fire was evidently arrested.
Every now and then a jet of flame shot up to the sky;

a few more minutes of fierce exertion and the enemy
was got under, and Wilton descended from his post
of observation to find a new authority on the scene,
who was bustling about very actively. This was the
master of a small station about half a mile farther up
the line, scarcely to be seen from the fast and express
trains, which never stopped there, but elevated by
the present catastrophe into importance and authority.
By his directions the guard and stoker, who were
most injured, were removed to a small town at a little
distance, where medical aid could be procured. Having discovered and liberated his yelping dog, Wilton
sought what information he could from this official.

"No, sir; there ain't much damage done. The
stoker of the ballast train is hurt a good deal; but the
guard is more stunned than hurt. No lives lost,
thank God—only some bruises and a broken head.
You see, it's getting late for night-travelling, and there
wasn't a soul in the first carriage. How did it happen? You see, the ballast train was shunted here to
wait till yours was past; but those pointsmen are
overworked, and this here forgot to set back the
points; so you see, right into the other engine,"
etc., etc.

After mixing with the other passengers, and ascertaining what they intended to do, or if he could be
of any use to them, Wilton bethought him of his lonely

little travelling companion, and returned to seek her. She had advanced nearer the scene of action, and climbed up the low bank which here bordered the line, the better to see what was going on.

"I am afraid you must think I was not coming back," said Wilton, offering his hand to help her down.

"I saw you were well occupied," she said, touching it lightly as she descended.

"By Jove! you are shivering with cold—and no wonder, without a cloak or plaid! Wait for a moment and I will bring you mine from our carriage."

"Would you also be so kind as to bring my bonnet and a small travelling bag? I should have gone for them myself, only I could hardly stand."

But Wilton was gone, and returned quickly. "There are but three other ladies," he said, assisting to wrap his plaid around her, "and they are going up to a small town or village about two miles off, to rest at the inn ; and when they are refreshed, intend posting on to their destination, which is somewhere in this district. Would you like to go with them, or wait at a little station close to this, where a fresh train will be sent as soon as they can clear the line?"

"Oh, I will go to the station. I am anxious to get on as soon as possible."

"And so am I. I shall, therefore, remain there also, and shall be most happy to be of any use to you."

"Thank you. Can I walk to this station at once?"

"Certainly, if you will take my arm."

"I feel I must to steady myself," she replied. "I did not know I was so much frightened and shaken. I feel ashamed."

They walked on in silence for a few yards, and then Wilton asked if she was going much farther.

"Yes," with a sigh, "a long way—over the Border to a place called Monkscleugh."

"Indeed!" cried Wilton; "that is my destination also."

She made no reply, and they accomplished the short distance in silence, save for a few friendly remarks and inquiries from Wilton. The station was almost deserted when they reached it; but the gaslight and a good fire were very welcome; and the station master soon returned with the intelligence that they had collected more men, who were working hard to clear the line, and, that, as soon as it was passable, a fresh train would be sent on from A——.

The station-master was a short man—broad without being stout—with a peculiarly weather-beaten aspect, his mouth screwed to one side, and one eye squeezed down to the other, as if in the habit of facing the sun's glare without adequate shelter. He spoke, too, in a *staccato* style, as if some intermittent power pumped up his words.

"I dare say this lady would be glad of a cup of tea or something," said Wilton, looking compassionately at the figure of his companion, who had drawn a chair to the fire, and sat down wearily, putting a small, well-booted foot upon the fender.

"I have sent up to the village for refreshments, sir ; but I am sorry to say I have nothing in the place. I generally go away for my meals."

So saying, the station-master hurried off.

"I do not feel to want anything but sleep," said the lady. "I have not had any for many nights, and I am scarce awake now. If I could but close my eyes, and rest."

She raised them as she spoke to Wilton—such large, black-blue eyes, so heavy with fatigue, that his compassion for her evident exhaustion was naturally increased by the admiration they excited.

"You really ought to take something, if we could get it," he said. "Such a shock must have been too much for you, though you showed remarkable pluck."

"Yet I was dreadfully frightened," she replied, clasping her hands over one knee, and gazing dreamily into the fire. "I do not fear death so much as being hurt and helpless."

"Well," said Wilton, cheerfully, "we must find a resting-place for you. There ought to be a lady's waiting-room even here." He rose and looked about as he spoke. "And so there is "—he opened a door on the right of the fireplace—"a very desolate-looking chamber. Still there is an uneasy-looking stuffed bench, and perhaps, with my cloak and plaid, you might manage to get an hour's sleep while we are waiting."

"How good of you to think of all this!" she exclaimed, looking at him more attentively than she had yet done. "But it is dark—and see! the lock is broken. I do not think I should like to sleep with an open door."

"Let me light the gas," said Wilton, turning the stiff tap and striking one of his fusees. "Now the only objection is the broken lock. I will mount guard outside, and, trust me, no one shall intrude upon you. What do you say?"

"Many, many thanks. I will gladly lie down and try to sleep. Are *you* not weary?"

"Not in the least. I would advise your trying to compose yourself at once; the others will be here soon, and will probably talk and make a row. By-the-way," interrupting himself, "would you like to telegraph to your friends that you are all right? I am going to do so myself."

"Telegraph to my friends!" she replied, stopping and looking full at him, her large, dark, dewy eyes lighting up as a half-sad, half scornful smile dimpled

her cheek. " It is not at all necessary ; they will not
distress themselves."

She bent her head as Wilton held the door for her
to pass through. Closing it after her, he returned to
his seat by the fire, wondering at himself; for, though
far too manly a man to adopt a tone of selfish indifference toward others, though he would have shown
kindly consideration to a plain or an elderly woman
in such circumstances, he was conscious of an extraordinary degree of interest and admiration for his quiet,
undemonstrative fellow-traveller. She was so gentle,
yet so indifferent ; so simple and so self-possessed ;
evidently grateful to him for his attentions, and yet
utterly regardless of him as a " good-looking fellow,"
or as anything save a civil travelling-companion.
There was something marvellously attractive in the
almost infantine sweetness of her mouth and delicate
chin, and the contrast of her earnest, expressive eyes.

" Who can she be ? " asked Wilton of himself;
" though quite unconventional, there is a high tone
about her, poor little thing ! It is as well she fell in
with such a steady fellow as myself. I must see her
safe to the end of her journey, and find out all about
her before we part."

His reflections were interrupted by an influx of
some of the passengers, who now began to collect,
having impeded the efforts of the railway officials as

much as possible by their attempts to afford assist-
ance ; they were all exceedingly talkative and hungry,
not to say hilarious, from the reaction of their escape.
The refreshments which had been sent for had now
arrived, and the little station looked quite crowded.
In the midst of the buzz of voices, while all except
Wilton were gathered round the table discussing the
viands placed thereon, he observed the door of the
ladies' room open gently and his *prot'g'* appear, his
cloak over one shoulder, and trailing behind. Wilton
immediately went toward her.

"I cannot sleep," she said ; "I dozed a little just
at first, but now I am quite awake and restless."

"That's bad," returned Wilton. "Will you come
in here and sit by the fire ?"

"Oh no !" shrinking back, "not among all those
people."

"Well, it would not be very pleasant ; but shall
you not be very cold ?"

"Not if you will still allow me to have your cloak."

"Certainly; and I hope we shall not be kept
much longer. Could we not get you a fire here?" and
he walked in unceremoniously.

"I do not think even you could manage that," she
returned, with a quiet smile, as she placed herself at
a table under the gaslight, and opened a large note-
book, as if about to make some entries.

"Not a strong-minded female taking notes, I hope," thought Wilton. "She is far too pretty for that."

"No," said he, aloud, as he observed there was no fireplace. "With all the will imaginable, I cannot manage a fire; but can I do nothing more? I must insist on your taking some wine or tea. They are all devouring out there; and I have had some very tolerable brandy-and-water myself," and Wilton beckoned a waiter to bring some refreshment.

"I tell you what you could do for me," said the young lady, suddenly looking up more brightly than she had yet done; "make the station-master come in here and talk—ask him questions. Oh, you know what I mean!" she went on, with a sort of graceful petulance as Wilton looked at her in no small surprise, "anything to make him talk. There, I think I hear him in the next room; please to watch for him and bring him here. I will begin, you can follow me; when I say 'thank you,' send him away—there, please to catch him."

Wilton, greatly wondering that the first signs of animation in his interesting companion should be aroused by so rugged and commonplace a subject, hastened to obey, and soon returned with the functionary.

"Oh!" said the lady, bending her head with such

a proud yet gracious air that the man involuntarily removed his hat. "Pray tell me, is there really no serious injury? I should be more satisfied were I assured by you."

"Well, mum, I am happy to say there is no one much hurt to speak of," etc., etc.

"Is it long since you have had an accident before?" asked Wilton, not very well knowing how to proceed in compliance with a little private imperative nod from the fair inquisitor.

The question was opportune, for it launched the station-master upon quite a flood of memories into which he rushed and talked for good ten minutes without intermission. How long he would have continued it is impossible to say, but one of the porters came to call him, as there was a telegraph from ——.

Wilton followed to hear the news, and returned, after a short absence, with the intelligence that the expected train would not arrive for another hour.

"That is long." replied the young lady, scarce lifting her head; then, as Wilton, a little mortified by her tone, turned to leave the room, she exclaimed, still looking down, "Stay one moment, if not inconvenient."

"Certainly," and Wilton stood still for another minute or two.

"There," she said, holding out the book, "is that like him?"

Wilton took it and uttered an exclamation of surprise. On the page before him was a bold, rapid, admirable sketch of the station-master; all the characteristic lines and puckers were there, but slightly idealized.

"This is first-rate! You are quite an artist."

"I wish I was! Let me touch it a little more. What a capital face it is—so rugged, so humorous—yet so English; not the least bit picturesque. I shall work this into something some day."

"Then I am right in supposing you an artist? May I look again?" said Wilton, sitting down beside her.

"Oh, yes; you may look at my scratchings. This is my note-book. I like to draw everything—but, you see, most imperfectly."

"I do not, indeed. I know very little of art, though I can sketch roughly—merely professional work—but you seem to me to have both genius and skill."

"Some taste, scarce any skill."

There was something quite genuine in her tone—not the least tinge of mock-modesty—as she turned over the pages, and touched them here and there, while her manner was singularly devoid of coquetry. Wilton might have been her grandfather for all of embarrassment or excitement his attentions caused.

"And you can draw; perhaps you know these trees; they are not far from Monkscleugh."

She showed him a group of beeches most delicately yet clearly drawn.

"I do not know the neighborhood. I am going there for the first time. May I ask if you reside there?"

"Yes, at present. Oh, you will find a great deal to sketch all about—especially by the river—and there is beauty, too, in the gray skies and rich brown moors; but how unlike the beauty of the sunny south!"

"It is not necessary to ask which you like; your voice tells that," said Wilton.

"And are you not fond of drawing?" she resumed, as if the subject had an irresistible attraction.

"You would not look at such school-boy productions as mine," returned Wilton, smiling. "As I said before, they are mere rough professional drawings."

"Professional! What is your profession?"

This rather leading question was put with the most straightforward simplicity.

"I am a soldier."

"A soldier!"—looking very earnestly at him—"what a pity!"

"Why?" asked Wilton, surprised, and a little nettled. "Soldiers are necessary evils."

"But what evils! what symbols of deeper evils

2

than themselves ! I do not mean to say," interrupting herself with a sudden consciousness that her words were rude, while a delicate tinge of color came and went in her cheek, " that *you* are bad or wicked ; but it is so sad to think that such things, or people rather, should be necessary still."

"No doubt it would be better for the world to be in an Arcadian or paradisiacal condition ; but, as it is, I am afraid it will be a long time before we can dispense with fighting or fighting-men. However, you are right—war is a horrible thing, and I hope we shall have no more for a long time."

" Alas ! how dare we hope that, so long as it is in the power of three or four men to plunge three or four nations into such horrors ? "

"Ah, I see I have encountered a dangerous democrat," said Wilton, laughing ; and, vaguely pleased to see her drawn out of her cool composure, he watched the varying color in her cheek while she was turning over the leaves of her sketch-book, seeming to seek for something. " Pardon me," said Wilton, after waiting for a reply, and determined to speak again, " but I imagine you are not English."

" I scarcely know—yes, I believe I am." She spoke in her former quiet tone again.

" In England all young ladies are conservative, at least all I have ever known," continued Wilton.

" Conservative !—I have read that word often in the journals. Is it legitimacy, Church and state, and all that ? "

" Exactly."

" Well, the young ladies I know—and they are but few—are very charming, very accomplished ; but they know nothing, absolutely nothing. Is it not strange ? "

There was not the slightest approach to cynicism in her tone, but she looked at Wilton as if fully expecting him to share her wonder.

" Is this the character of the young ladies of the unknown land into which I am about to plunge ? I fancied Scotchwomen were educated within an inch of their lives."

" I know English girls best. Some are very learned ; have been taught quantities ; they can tell the very year when printing was tried, and when Queen Elizabeth first wore silk stockings, and when every great pope was born ; and they read French and German ; and oh, I cannot tell all they can do and say. And yet—yet, they know nothing—they care for nothing—they lead such strange lives."

" I suppose the lives of all girls are much alike," observed Wilton, more and more curious to find out some leading acts concerning his rather original companion. " But, as we are both bound for the same place, perhaps I may have some opportunity of com-

municating my observations on the intellectual status
of the Monkscleugh young ladies?"

"There is very little probability of such an event,"
said she, with an amused smile.

"Then you do not reside at Monkscleugh?"

"Within three miles of it."

"I am going down to a shooting-lodge called
Glenraven," hoping she would respond by naming her
own abode.

"Indeed! I know it; there are some lovely bits
about there."

"We shall be neighbors, then?"

"Yes, in a certain sense. Here," she continued,
turning over a fresh page of her book, "this is the
outline of a very lovely brae and burn close to your
abode."

It was only a bit of broken bank; a stream, dotted
with stones, lay below, with some mountain ash trees
spreading their feathery foliage against the sky; but
there were wonderful grace and beauty in the sketch.
"This gives you a very faint idea of the reality," she
resumed, in a low, soft tone, as if inwardly contem-
plating it. "The water is clear brown; it foams and
chafes round these large black stones, and all sorts
of delicious mosses and leaves lurk below the edge;
and then ferns wave about the rocks on the brae, and
there are gleams of purple heather and tufts of green,

green grass, and behind here a great, wild, free hill-side. Oh, it is so quiet and dreamy there—delicious!"

"And this delightful brae is near the lodge?" said Wilton, when she paused, after listening an instant in hopes she would speak on, there was such caressing sweetness in her voice."

"No, not very near; almost a mile away, I think." She evidently knew the place well.

"I hope you will continue to transfer the beauties of Glenraven after I become a dweller there."

"Oh, yes; whenever I have time; to draw is my greatest pleasure."

With all her frankness, he was not an inch nearer the discovery of her actual abode.

"I suppose you do not live far from the scene of your sketch?"

"Not far: Brosedale is quite a mile and a half on this side," touching the page with her pencil; "and the pathway to Monkscleugh goes over the brae."

"Indeed! I imagine I have heard the name of Brosedale before."

"Very likely; it is, I believe, the largest gentle-man's seat in the neighborhood."

"Yes, yes; I remember now: it belongs to Sir Peter Fergusson."

"Exactly."

"She cannot be his daughter," thought Wilton;

" I suppose she must be the governess.—I understand he is quite the grand seigneur of Monkscleugh," he said aloud.

"Well, I suppose so. He is a good little man—at least, whenever I see him he is very kind." After some further, but intermittent conversation, there was a sort of movement in the next room, and Wilton's companion begged him to go and see what was the matter.

The matter was the arrival of the promised engine and train; so Wilton's conversation and inquiries were put an end to for the present.

To his infinite disgust, when they resumed their places, a fat elderly man, a commercial traveller from Glasgow, intruded upon their *tête-à-tête*, and absorbed all the talk to himself. He was great in railway experiences, accidents included, and addressed a steady, unceasing flow of talk to Wilton, who burned to eject him summarily from the window.

The young lady had sunk to sleep at last, carefully wrapped in Wilton's cloak, and the bagman, having exhausted either his powers or his subject, composed himself to slumber. But Wilton could not rest for a long time, and he seemed hardly to have lost consciousness before they stopped at Carlisle. Here the commercial traveller alighted, and Wilton's puzzling companion woke up.

"We shall be at Monkscleugh in three-quarters of an hour," said Wilton; "can I be of any further use to you if your friends are not there to meet you, as may be the case?"

"There will be no friends to meet me," she replied; "but I need trouble you no more: I go to the house of one of the Brosedale employés, who will send me on."

"After a hair-breadth 'scape, such as ours," said Wilton, amused at his own unwonted bashfulness and difficulty in putting the question, "may I ask the name of my comrade in danger?"

"My name?" with some surprise. "Oh, Ella— Ella Rivers."

"And mine; do you not care to inquire?" said Wilton, bending forward to look into her eyes.

"Yes," she said, slowly, with a slight sigh; "what is your name?"

"Wilton."

"Have you no other?—there is always more character in a Christian name."

"Mine is Ralph."

"Ralph—Ralph—I do not seem to understand it. Are you noble?"

"No; simply Colonel Wilton."

"Ah! a colonel is higher than a captain, and lower than a general?"

"Just so."

She relapsed into silence, scarcely responding to Wilton's endeavor to make her talk and turn her eyes upon him. He was surprised to find himself counting the minutes that remained before he should be compelled to lose sight of his curiously fascinating companion. The parting moment came all too quickly, and Wilton was obliged to say "Good-by."

"I hope to have the pleasure of seeing you again," he said, politely.

"There is nothing so unlikely," she returned, with a slight blush; "but," holding out her hand, "your kindness will always be a pleasant recollection."

She bowed and turned away so decidedly that Wilton felt he must not follow.

CHAPTER III.

MAJOR MONCRIEF was as good as his word, and joined his friend before the stipulated ten days had expired. Nor had time hung heavily on Wilton's hands. He was up early, and turned out every day to tramp through the heather, or among the wooded valleys of the picturesque country surrounding the lodge. He was an active pedestrian and a good shot; moreover, he went thoroughly into the pursuit or amusement that engaged him. The game-keeper pronounced him a real sportsman, but thought it rather odd that, whatever line of country they had beaten, or were going to beat, Colonel Wilton generally contrived to pass across the brae, or the path leading from Brosedale to Monkscleugh. The evening was generally spent in arranging and correcting his Crimean and Indian diaries, so, with the help of a couple of horses, which arrived under the care of his soldier servant, he had no lack of amusement and occupation. Nevertheless, he welcomed Moncrief very warmly.

" You are a first-rate fellow for joining me so soon.

It certainly is not good for man to live alone. These are capital quarters—lots of game, beautiful country, hospitable neighbors. Look here! I found these when I came in yesterday."

So spoke Wilton, handing a card and a note to his friend as they drew near the fire after dinner.

" Hum !—ah!—Sir Peter, or rather Lady Fergusson has lost no time," returned the major, laying down the card, which was inscribed " Sir Peter J. Fergusson, Brosedale," and, opening the note, which bore a crest and monogram in lilac and gold, " her ladyship is anxious we should partake of the hospitality of Brosedale on Thursday next, ' *sans cérémonie.*' I am to bring my friend Colonel Wilton."

"Who are these people?" asked Wilton, as he peeled a walnut.

"Oh, Sir Peter is a man who made a big fortune in China ; a very decent little fellow. He married an Honorable widow with a string of daughters, who manages a happy amalgamation of her old and her new loves by styling herself the Honorable Lady Fergusson. Sir Peter bought a large estate here for a song when the Grits of Brosedale smashed up. I met the baronet in London at General Maclellan's, and my lady was monstrously civil ; hoped to see me when I was in their neighborhood, and all that ; but, of course, Wilton, you will not go? We did not come down here for polite society—it would be a bore."

Wilton did not answer immediately. "I do not know," he said, at last. "It would not do to give such near neighbors the cold shoulder. We might be glad of them if we tire of each other. Suppose we go this time, and see what sort of neighbors we have?"

Moncrief looked at his friend with some surprise. "As you like," he said. "I should have thought it anything but a temptation to you."

"My dear fellow, the weather and the sport and the scenery have made me so confoundedly amiable that I am indisposed to say 'No' to any one."

"Very well, I will write and accept; but if you think I am going to dine with every resident who chooses to enliven his dulness by entertaining two such choice spirits as ourselves, you are very much mistaken, my lad. I suppose you are anxious to prosecute your search for a wife, in obedience to that crotchety old peer."

"Not I," returned Wilton, laughing; "and, if I were, I do not think it very likely I should find the desired article among the Honorable Lady Fergusson's daughters."

"I believe Fergusson was married before," said the major, "in his earlier, humbler days, when he little thought he would reign in the stead of old Jammie

Grits at Brosedale." Whereupon the major branched off into some local anecdotes, which he told with much dry humor. Wilton listened and laughed, but did not forget to put him in mind of the necessary reply to Lady Fergusson's invitation.

The major was by no means well pleased at being obliged to dress after a severe day's work, for which he was not as yet in training; moreover, he was full . fifteen years older than his friend, and at no period of his life possessed the fire, the eager energy which Wilton carried with him into every pursuit, even into every whim. So he grumbled through the purgatorial operation, and marvelled gloomily at Wilton's unusual readiness to rush into the inanities of a country dinner.

As to Wilton, he felt quite angry with himself for the curious elation with which he mounted the dog-cart that was to convey them to Brosedale. He did not think there was so much boyish folly left in him ; but, occupy himself as he might, he could not banish the haunting eyes of Ella Rivers. He could not forget the unconscious dignity of her question, " Is it death ? " The full knowledge of danger, and yet no wild terror ! There was a fascination about that insignificant stranger which, absurd and unreasonable though it was, he could not shake off. This effect was heightened by the peculiar, sad indifference of her manner. It was odd that he had never met her

in any of his varied and extensive excursions. The
weather had been beautiful, too—most favorable for
sketching, but she had never appeared. If he could
see her again, and disperse the species of mystery
which formed part of her charm, by ascertaining who
and what she was, he felt as if he could better break
the spell. But all this was more vaguely felt than
actually thought and acknowledged. Wilton would
have laughed at any one who told him that his
thoughts were all more or less pervaded by the quiet
little girl who had shown such an unusual dislike to
soldiers.

The friends reached Brosedale just as Sir Peter
hoped they would not be late. The house—which
was an old one, so largely added to, altered, and im-
proved, that scarcely any of the original could be
traced—was very like all rich men's houses where the
women have no distinctive taste—handsome, ornate,
and commonplace. Lady Fergusson was a fine, well-
preserved woman, richly dressed in silk and lace.
She received Major Moncrief and his friend with
much cordiality, and presented them to her daughters,
Miss Helen and Miss Gertrude Saville, and also to a
nephew and niece who were staying in the house.

"My eldest daughter, who was with me when we
had the pleasure of meeting you in town, is staying
with her aunt, Lady Ashleigh, in Wiltshire," said the

hostess to Moncrief. "She is quite enthusiastic about archæology, and Ashleigh is in itself a treasure of antiquity."

Miss Helen Saville was a grand, tall brunette, with rich red lips and cheeks, luxuriant if somewhat coarse black hair, and large, round black eyes, that looked every one and everything full in the face. Her sister was smaller, less dark, and in every way a faint copy of the great original. The niece was a plain girl, with good points, dressed effectively ; and the nephew a young lieutenant in some hussar regiment, who considered himself bound to fraternize with Wilton. The latter was told off to take in Miss Saville by Sir Peter, a small man, whose close-clipped white whiskers looked like mutton-chop patterns thickly floured. He had a quiet, not to say depressed air, and a generally dry-salted aspect, which made Wilton wonder, as he stood talking with him before the fire, at the stuff out of which the conquerors of fortune are sometimes made.

"What a beautiful country this is !" said Wilton to his neighbor, as his soup-plate was removed, and Ganymede, in well-fitting broadcloth, filled his glass.

"Strangers admire it, but it is by no means a good neighborhood."

"Indeed ! I suppose, then, you are driven in upon your own resources."

" Such as they are," with a smile displaying white but not regular teeth.

" No doubt they are numerous. Let me see ; what are a young lady's resources—crochet, croquet, and curates, healing the sick and feeding the hungry ? "

" Oh, I do none of those things. The crochet, croquet, and curates, are my sister's amusements, and I dislike both the sick and the hungry, although I have no objection to subscribe for them."

" Ah ! you are terribly destitute ; and you do not ride, or I should have met you."

" Yes, I am very fond of riding ; but we have scarcely returned a week, and I have had a bad cold."

" Perhaps you draw ? " asked Wilton, approaching his object from afar.

" No ; I have always preferred music. None of us care for drawing, except my youngest sister."

" Indeed ! " (looking across the table), " that is a pleasant variety from the crochet, croquet, and curates."

" No ; not Gertrude—I mean Isabel. She is still in the school-room."

" Ah ! And I suppose sketches with her governess ? "

" Yes."

" As I imagined," thought Wilton, " my pretty companion is the governess. Perhaps she will be in

the drawing-room when we go there. If so, I must lay
the train for some future meeting."

"Pray, Colonel Wilton, are you any relation to a
Mr. St. George Wilton we met at Baden last summer?
He was, or is, *attaché* somewhere."

"He has the honor of being my first cousin once
removed, or my third cousin twice removed—some
relation, at all events. I am not at all well up in the
ramifications of the family."

"Well, he is a very agreeable person, I assure you,
quite a favorite with every one, and speaks all sorts of
languages. There was a Russian princess at Baden,
quite wild about him."

"Is it possible? These fair barbarians are impressionable, however. I have met the man you
mention years ago. We were at that happy period
when one can relieve the overburdened heart by a
stand-up fight, and I have a delightful recollection of
thrashing him."

Miss Saville laughed, and then said, "I hope you
will be better friends when you meet again. I believe
he is coming here next week."

"Oh, I promise to keep the peace—unless, indeed, I see him greatly preferred before me," returned Wilton, with a rather audacious look, which
by no means displeased Miss Saville, who was of the
order of young ladies that prefer a bold wooer.

While the talk flowed glibly at Sir Peter's end of the table, Lady Fergusson was delicately cross-examining Moncrief as to the social standing of his friend.

"Try a little melon, Major Moncrief. Pray help yourself. That port is, I believe, something remarkable. And you were saying Colonel Wilton is related to that curious old Lord St. George. We met a cousin of his—his heir, in fact—abroad last year, a very charming young man."

"Not his heir, Lady Fergusson, for my friend Ralph is the heir. I am quite sure of that."

"Indeed!" returned Lady Fergusson, blandly. "I dare say you are right;" and her countenance assumed a softer expression while she continued to bestow most flattering attentions upon the rather obtuse major.

The after-dinner separation seemed very long to Wilton, although he was a good deal interested by his host's observations upon Eastern matters; for Sir Peter was a shrewd, intelligent man; but at last they joined the ladies, and found their numbers augmented by a little girl of twelve or thirteen, and a rigid lady in gray silk, who was playing a duet with Miss Gertrude Saville. Wilton betook himself, coffee-cup in hand, to Miss Saville, who was turning over a book of photographs in a conspicuously-disengaged position.

4

"I have had quite an interesting disquisition with your father on the East and China. He evidently knows his subject."

"Sir Peter is not my father," said the young lady, with a tinge of haughtiness.

"True. I forgot," apologetically. "Ah! that is your little artist-sister. I am very fond of children."

"Are you? I am sure I am not, little tiresome, useless animals."

"Human nature in the raw, eh!"

"Yes; I prefer it dressed. Still, to quote an inelegant proverb, 'Too much cookery spoils the broth!' But some is quite essential. Here, Isabel, take my cup." The little girl approached and offered to take Wilton's.

"No, not at any age could I permit such a thing," said he, laughing. "And so you are the artist in the house of Saville! Are you very fond of drawing?"

"I used not to be until—" she began to reply, when her sister interrupted her.

"Look, Isabel, Miss Walker wants you. Miss Walker (Hooky Walker, as my Cousin Jim calls her, because she has a hooked nose) is the governess. I think poor Isabel is a little afraid of her. She is awfully clever, and very slow."

Wilton looked at her in deep disappointment; the mystery was growing more difficult. Perhaps after all, Ella Rivers did *not* live at Brosedale ! Now he recalled all she had said, he found she had not positively asserted that she lived there, or anywhere. Could it be possible that she had slipped from his grasp—that he would never see her again—was she only the wraith of a charming, puzzling girl ? Pooh! what was it to him ? His business was to enjoy three or four months' sport and relaxation. He was so far fortunate. His chum, Moncrief, had pitched on excellent shooting-quarters for their joint occupation. His campaign had proved a very remedial measure, for he was quite clear of his debts, and the good intentions of Lord St. George formed a pleasing if uncertain perspective. So Wilton reflected, while Miss Helen Saville performed a *tarantella* of marvellous difficulty, where accidentals, abstruse harmonious discords, and double shakes, appalled the listening ear. When it was finished, the audience were properly complimentary, which homage the fair performer disregarded with a cool and lofty indifference highly creditable to her training in the school of modern young-ladyism.

"What an amount of study must be required to attain such skill !" said Wilton, as she returned to her seat near him. " Is it indiscreet to ask how many hours a day it took to produce all that ? "

"Oh, not so very many. When I was in the

school-room, I practised four or five ; now much less keeps me in practice. Are you fond of music, Colonel Wilton ?"

"Yes, I am extremely fond of it, in an ignorant way. I like old ballads, and soft airs, and marches, and all that low style of music suited to outside barbarians like myself." And Wilton, instinctively conscious that the brilliant Miss Saville admired him, bestowed a mischievous glance upon her as he spoke, not sorry, perhaps, to act upon the well-known principle of counter-irritation, to cure himself of the absurd impression made upon him by his chance encounter.

"I understand," returned Miss Saville, a little piqued, as he had intended she should be. "You look upon such compositions as I have just played as a horrid nuisance."

"Like a certain very bad spirit, I tremble and adore," said Wilton, laughing. "I have no doubt however, that you could charm my savage breast, or rouse my martial fire, with 'Auld Robin Gray' or 'Scots wha hae wi' Wallace bled.'"

"No, I cannot," replied Miss Saville, haughtily. "Gertrude sings a little, and, I believe, can give you 'Auld Robin Gray,' if you ask her."

"I shall try, at all events," said Wilton, amused at the slight annoyance of her tone, and rising to execute his purpose, when Helen, to his surprise, forestalled him by calling her sister to her very amiably, "Gertrude, will you sing for Colonel Wilton? I will play your accompaniment." So the desired ballad was sung, very correctly and quite in tune, but as if performed by some vocal instrument utterly devoid of human feeling.

There was more music, and a good deal of talk about hunting arrangements ; but Wilton was extremely pleased to be once more in the dog-cart, cigar in mouth, facing the fresh, brisk breeze, on their homeward way. The major, on the contrary, was in a far more happy frame of mind than at starting. He preferred hunting to shooting, and was highly pleased at the prospect of two days' hunting a week.

"You are right, Moncrief," said Wilton, as they bowled away over the smooth, hard road ; "these country dinners and family parties ought to be devoutly avoided by all sensible men."

"I do not know," returned the mentor. "I think they are a very tolerable lot ; and I fancy you found amusement enough with that slashing fine girl—you took very little notice of any one else, by Jove ! I sometimes think I hate the lassies, they are such kittle cattle. Now, a woman that's 'wooed and married and a' ' is safe, and may be just as pleasant."

" I acknowledge the fact, but I object to the morality," returned Wilton, laughing.

" You do ?   I was not aware of your regeneration."

" Hallo ! " cried Wilton. " There's some one in front there, just under the shadow of that beech-tree."

" Yes, I thought I saw something. It's a child or a girl."

Wilton, who was driving, did not answer, though he drew up suddenly, and made a movement as if to throw aside the plaid that wrapped his knees and spring down.

" What are you about ? are you daft, man ? "

" Nothing, nothing.   I fancied—here, Byrne, look at this trace ; it is loose."

" Sure it's all right, sir."

" Is it ?   Never mind."   And Wilton, after casting an eager look up a pathway which led from the beech-tree into the grounds of Brosedale, gathered up the reins and drove rapidly home.

It was about a week after the Brosedale dinner that Wilton had sallied forth, intending to ride over to Monkscleugh.   He had nearly resigned the idea of ever encountering his fair fellow-traveller again, though he could not shake off the conviction that the slight dim figure which had flitted from out the shade of the beech-tree, across the moonlight, and into the gloom of the Brosedale plantations, was that of Miss Rivers. Still, it was most strange that she should be there at such an hour—half-past ten at least—rather too enterprising for a young lady. Yet, if Moncrief had not been with him, he would certainly have given chase, and satisfied himself as to the identity of the child or woman who had crossed their path.

On this particular afternoon, however, Wilton's thoughts were occupied by the letters he had received that morning, one of which was from Lord St. George, who wrote to remind him of his promise to call when he passed through London again. The viscount also mentioned that a former friend of his, the Earl of D——, would be in his (Wilton's) neighborhood early in November, and would probably call upon him.

Wilton smiled as he read this, remembering that the earl had three unmarried daughters. " A young gentleman," the writer continued, " calling himself St. George Wilton, left a card here some days ago, and was good enough to say that he would call again, which enabled me to forbid his admittance. He did repeat the attempt, when he told my valet, whom he asked to see, that he was going to Scotland, and would probably see Colonel Wilton, if I had any commands. I imagine my obliging namesake is a son of Fred Wilton, who was in the navy—but not exactly the type of an honest, simple sailor. I would advise you not to be on too cousinly terms. I have heard, even in my cell, of the young gentleman's diplomatic astuteness."

Pondering on this epistle, and smiling at the sudden interest evinced toward him by the eccentric peer, Wilton rode leisurely toward Monkscleugh, enjoying the splendid golden evening tinge in the sky, the rich and varied hues of wood and moorland, when a sudden turn in the road brought him face to face with a slight, gray figure, wearing a wide-brimmed hat, and carrying a small parcel. In an instant all the half-scorned but potent longings, the vivid picture-like recollections of tones and glances, that had haunted him even while he laughed at himself for being pervaded by them—all these absurd fancies he had so nearly shaken off rushed back in a torrent, and made his pulses leap at the immediate prospect of solving many mysteries.

He was dismounted and at her side in an instant. " I thought you had vanished—that I had lost you forever ! " he exclaimed, with the sort of well-bred impetuosity peculiar to his manner ; while, seeing that she made no motion to hold out her hand, he only lifted his hat.

The faint color came to her cheek as she raised her eyes frankly to his, with a brighter, merrier smile than he had seen upon her lip before. "Neverthe-less, I have not been very far away."

"Have you been at Brosedale all the time—then how is it we have not met?"

"I cannot tell; but I have been at Brosedale."

Wilton threw the reins over his arm, and walked on beside her. "And are you all right again—recovered from your fright, and had sleep enough?" looking at her eagerly as he spoke, and noting the soft lustre of her eyes, the clear, pale cheek, the ripe red though not full lips, all so much fairer and fresher than when they parted.

"Yes, I am quite well, and rested." A pause. She was apparently not inclined to talk more than she could help.

"Do you know I quite expected to see you when I dined at Brosedale the other day—how was it you did not appear?"

"What! did you expect to see me at dinner? Do you, then, think I am a much-disguised princess?"

"Not so very much disguised," he replied, rather surprised at her tone.

She raised her eyes fully to his, with a look half amused, half scornful. "You might dine many times at Brosedale without seeing me. Do you know that Sir Peter Fergusson was married before, and he has one son—a poor, crippled, often-suffering boy of thirteen, I think? Well, this boy can do very little to amuse himself; he does not care for study, but he loves pictures and drawing, so I was engaged about a year ago to be, not his governess—I am too ignorant—nor his companion—that would be a lady-in-waiting—but a *souffre douleur* and teacher of drawing. I live with my poor boy, who is never shown to visitors; and we are not unhappy together."

"I have heard of this son, but thought he was away; and you are always with him—very fortunate for him, but what a life for you!"

"A far better life than many women have," she replied, softly, looking away from him and speaking as if to herself.

"Still, it is an awful sacrifice!"

She laughed with real, sweet merriment. "That depends on what has been sacrificed. And you," she went on, with the odd independence of manner which, had her voice been less soft and low, her bearing less gentle, might have seemed audacious, "do you like Glenraven? Have you found many lovely bits of scenery?"

"I am charmed with the country; and, were I as fortunate as young Fergusson in a companion, I might even try my 'prentice hand at sketching."

"If you will not try alone, neither will you even if Claude Lorraine came to cut your pencils."

" I wish," said Wilton, " I had a chance of cutting yours."

" But you have not," she returned, with a sort of indolent gravity not in the least coquettish, and a pause ensued. Wilton had seldom felt so adrift with any woman ; perfectly frank and ready to talk, there was yet a strange half-cold indifference in her manner that did not belong to her fair youth, and upon which he dared not presume, though he chafed inwardly at the mask her frankness offered.

" I suppose you are kept very much in the house with your—pupil ? " asked Wilton.

" Sometimes ; he has been very unwell since I came back. But he has a pony-carriage, and he drives about, and I drive it occasionally ; but it pains him to walk, poor fellow ! He is interested in some things. He wished much to see you and hear about the Crimea and India."

" I am sure," cried Wilton, with great readiness, " I should be most happy to see him or contribute to his amusement—pray tell him so from me."

" No, I cannot," with a shake of the head ; " Lady Fergusson is so very good she thinks everything wrong ; and to walk upon a country-road with a great man like you would be worse than wrong—it would be shocking ! "

Wilton could not refrain from laughing at the droll

gravity of her tone, though in some indefinable way it piqued and annoyed him.

"Well, they are all out of the way—they have driven over to A——. Have they not?"

"Yes, and therefore there was no one to send to Monkscleugh to choose some prints that Donald wanted very much for a screen we are making, so I went."

"And so at last I had the pleasure of meeting you. I had begun to fear I should never have a chance of asking if you had recovered from your fright; for though no woman could have shown more pluck, you must have been frightened."

"I was, indeed, and I do not think I am naturally brave; but I must bid you good-morning—my way lies through the plantations."

"No, no! you must not send me adrift—are we not comrades? We have faced danger together; and I am sure you are not influenced by Lady Fergusson's views."

"Lady Fergusson! pooh!"

There was wonderful, airy, becoming grace in the pant which seemed to blow defiance like a kiss to the immaculate Lady Fergusson. "Nevertheless, I must say good-by, for your horse could not get through that."

She pointed to a small swing-gate, which led from

the road to a path across a piece of rough heath-
grown ground, between the road and the woods.

"Do you forbid me to escort you farther?" said
Wilton, quickly.

She thought an instant. "Were I going to walk
along the road I should not," the faintest color stealing over her cheek as she spoke; "it is pleasant to
talk with a new person sometimes, but I cannot alter
my route."

Wilton laughed, and, mounting rapidly, rode to the
farther side of the wide waste border, where there was
almost a small common; rousing up his horse he
rushed him at the fence separating Sir Peter's land
from the road, and landed safely within the boundary
just as his companion passed through the gate.

She gave a slight suppressed scream, and as he
again dismounted and joined her she looked very pale.

"How could you be so foolish as to do so!" she
exclaimed, almost angry. "You have frightened me."

"I am extremely sorry, but you can know little of
country-life; any man accustomed to hunt, and tolerably mounted, could have done as much."

She shook her head and walked on in silence,
most embarrassing to Wilton. "I hope I have not
displeased you," he said, earnestly, trying to look into
her eyes; "but I thought I had your permission to
accompany you a little farther."

"Yes, but who could imagine you would commit such an eccentricity as to take a leap like that?"

"I do not allow it was an eccentricity; I suppose you absolve me?"

"*Absolvo te!*—and the horse also. What a beautiful horse; how gently he follows you! I should so much like to sketch him; I fear I do not sketch animals well; I do not catch their character. Oh! could I sketch him now!" stopping short, and speaking with great animation. "Ah! I am too unreasonable—how could I ask you?"

The faint flitting flush that gave so much charm to her countenance, the sudden lighting up of her dark eyes with childlike eagerness, so unlike their usual expression of rather sad indifference, fascinated Wilton strangely; it was an instant before he replied, "Of course you shall sketch him; I have nothing to do, and am very glad to be of any service to you."

"Thank you, thank you very much! See," as she hastily unfolded her parcel, "I had just bought a new sketch-book, and you have provided a frontispiece." She seated herself on one of the large gray stones that dotted the piece of ground they were crossing, and quickly pointed a pencil. "There, turn his head a little toward me—not quite so much; that will do."

For some time Wilton stood still and silent, watching the small, white, deft fingers as they firmly and rapidly traced the outline, or put in the shading with broad, bold strokes ; occasionally he quieted the horse with a word, while he stored his memory with the pretty graceful figure, from a tiny foot half-buried in the soft, short grass to the well-set, haughty head and neck. " It is curious," he thought ; " here is a girl, in almost a menial position, with all the attributes of race, and a pair of eyes a king's daughter might pine to possess. Who can she be ? What is her history ? Why did she venture out alone when she ought to have been going to bed ? I shall ask her." These ideas passed through Wilton's brain, although any clear con- tinuity of thought was considerably impeded by the intermittent glimpses of a pair of full, deep-blue eyes, alternately upturned and downcast.

Suddenly Wilton was ordered, " Look away—over your horse's neck ; " and when, having preserved this position for several moments, he attempted to assume a more agreeable attitude, he was met with an eager " Pray be still for a little longer."

At last he was released.

" There," said his new acquaintance, " I will keep you no longer ; you have been very kind. See, how have I done it ? "

Wilton looked eagerly at the page held out to him.

" It is wonderfully good for so hasty a sketch," he said ; " the head and foreleg are capital, and as far as

I can judge, the likeness to the back of my head first-rate."

"I can generally catch the likeness of people," she returned, looking at the page and touching it here and there.

"Was that the reason you told me to look away?" asked Wilton, smiling.

"No; I did not wish your face in my book." Then, coloring and looking up, "Not that I forget your kindness to me. No; but, you understand, if Lady Fergusson found Mr.—that is, Colonel—Wilton's face in my book it would be the most shocking—the superlative shocking! Ah, there is no word enormous enough for such a 'shocking!'" And she laughed low but merrily. Wilton found it catching and laughed too, though it puzzled him to reply. She went on, "You would have come in better for the picture had you had your soldier's dress on, holding the horse and looking thus; and then, with some bright coloring, it might have been called 'On the Alert,' or some such thing, and sold for a hundred pence. I have seen this sort of sketches often in picture-shops." She spoke quickly, as if to cover a slight embarrassment, as she put away her pencils and book.

"Well, Miss Rivers, both Omar here and myself

will be most happy to sit, or rather stand, for you whenever you like."

"Ah, I shall never have another opportunity," she replied, walking toward the next fence and swing-gate, which led into the wood.

"You threatened as much when I bade you good-by, that I was never to see you again, and yet we have met; so I shall not be utterly downcast by your present prophecy."

She did not reply for a minute, and then exclaimed, "Suppose I were ever to succeed in making painting my career, would you, when you are a great nobleman —as Miss Saville says you will be—sit to me for your picture? And then we should have in the catalogue of the year's exhibition, 'Portrait of the Earl—or Duke—of Blank, by Ella Rivers.'"

"I can only say I will sit to you when and where you will."

"Ah, the possibility of independent work is too charming! But I forget myself—what o'clock is it?"

"Quarter to three," said Wilton, looking at his watch.

"Then I have been out too long. See how low the sun is! What glorious sunset hues! But I must not stay. Oh, how I hate to go in! How I love the liberty of the open air—the free, unwalled space! I feel another being in the prison of a great house. If you met me there, you would not know me. I should not dare to look up ; I should speak with bated breath, as if you were a superior. Can you fancy such a thing ? "

" No ; the wildest stretch of my imagination could not suggest such an idea. But can you not keep out a little longer ? " There was a strained, yearning look in her eyes that touched Wilton to the heart.

" Impossible ! My poor Donald will be cross and wretched. And you—you must go. I am foolish to have talked so much."

" You must let me come a little farther ; that fence up there is considerably stiffer than the last, but I think Omar will take it."

" No, no, no ! " clasping her hands.

" Yet you are not easily frightened. A young lady that can venture on a moonlight ramble when less adventurous people are going to bed must have strong nerves."

" Did you recognize me, then ? " she interrupted, not in the least disturbed by his question, but offering no explanation of her appearance at such an hour. " Yes, I am not cowardly in some things. However, I must say good morning."

" And you will not permit me come any farther ? "

" No ! "—He felt her " no " was very earnest.—

" Nay, more, I will stay here until I see you safe at the other side of that fence again."

There was a quaint, unembarrassed decision in her tone that somewhat lessened the pleasure with which he heard her.

" I assure you, it is not worth your while to watch so insignificant a feat of horsemanship ; that fence is a nothing."

" It does not seem so to me. It is possible an accident might happen, and then you would have no help. It would not be right to go on, and leave you to chance."

" If you will, then, I shall not keep you long. But, Miss Rivers, shall you not want to visit Monks-cleugh soon again? Have you abjured the pictur-esque braes of Glenraven? Is there no chance of another artistic talk with you?"

" No! Scarcely any possibility of such a thing. Good-by! I am much obliged for the sketch you granted me. My good wishes !"—a slight, proudly-gracious bend of the head—" but go!" She stood with her parcel tightly held, not the slightest symptom of a shake of the hand ; and, bold man of the world as he was, Wilton felt he must not presume to hold out his ; he therefore sprung into the saddle, and was soon over the fence and on the road. He raised his hat, and received a wave of the hand in return.

He remained there until she vanished through the
gate, and then, touching his impatient horse with the
heel, rode at speed to Monkscleugh, whence, having
accomplished his errand, he made a considerable
d.tour; so that evening had closed in, and the major
was waiting for dinner when he reached the lodge.

- "Where have you been?" demanded his hungry
senior. Wilton replied by an elaborate description of
his progress, *minus* the leading incident. The care he
took to mislead his friend and mask his own movements was surprising almost to himself. Yet, as he
reflected, what was there in the whole adventure to
conceal? No harm, certainly. Nor was Moncrief a
man who would jest coarsely, or draw wicked inferences. Still, it was impossible that he or any man
could understand the sort of impression Ella (it was
extraordinary how readily her name came to his mind)
had made upon him, unless he knew her; and even
then, what opinion would a cool, shrewd, common-
sense fellow like Moncrief form? He (Wilton) himself was, he feared, an impressionable idiot, and, no
doubt, exaggerated effects. Nevertheless, those soft,
deep eyes, with their earnest, yearning expression,
haunted him almost painfully. If he could see them
again, perhaps the effect would wear off; and, without thinking of the consequences, he most resolutely
determined to see her as soon as he could possibly

manage to do so, without drawing down any unpleas-
antness on that curious, puzzling, *piquante* girl. Major
Moncrief little imagined the vivid gleams of recollection and conjecture which ever and anon shot athwart
the current of his companion's ideas, as he took his
part in a discussion on the probable future of the
army in India with apparent interest, and even eagerness. The major's intelligence was keen so far as it
went, but that was not far ; therefore, though good
comrades and excellent friends, they seldom agreed
in opinion, Wilton's mental views being greatly wider :
the result of the difference being that Moncrief considered Wilton " a fine fellow, but deucedly visionary
—unpractical, in short," except in regimental matters ;
while Wilton spoke confidentially of the major as " a
capital old boy, but blind as a bat in some directions."

" Well, I maintain that we will never have such
men again as the soldiers and diplomates trained
under the old company. Why, even the officers of the
humbler grade—the Jacobs and Greens, to say nothing
of Edwards and a lot more—have very few equals in
the queen's service."

" True enough," replied Wilton, a little absently.
" We have too much pipe-clay and red-tape." So
spake he with his lips, while his brain was striving
busily to solve the question, " What could have brought
her out at night through the lonely woods ? Was it

possible that any motive less strong than an appointment with a lover could have braced a slight, nervous
girl (for, though plucky, she is nervous) to such an
undertaking? But, if she cared enough for any one
to dare it, it would be worth braving a good deal to
meet her." The picture suggested was rather fascinating, for the major exclaimed, " I say, Wilton, are you
asleep?" and brought their discussion to an end.

CHAPTER IV.

ANOTHER week passed rapidly over, assisted in its flight by two capital runs with the Friarshire hounds and a dinner at a neighboring magnate's, where Wilton made himself marvellously agreeable to Helen Saville, and promised to ride with her next day; but neither at luncheon nor in the house or grounds did he catch a glimpse of Ella Rivers ; again she had totally disappeared.

Miss Saville did not find Wilton so pleasant a companion, either during their ride or the luncheon which preceded it, as he had been at dinner the day before.

The accomplished Miss Walker and her pupil joined the party, but no other junior member of the family.

" What an infamous shame," thought Wilton, " not to let that poor boy have a little society ! " However, Fortune was not quite inexorable. As Wilton rode up to the door on their return, intending to bid the young ladies under his escort good-by, he became aware of a small figure, with a large head and prominent eyes, standing on the threshold, supported by crutches, while a pony-carriage was just disappearing toward the stables.

"What a nuisance!" said Helen to Gertrude. "I wonder what that boy wants?"

"Well, Donald, you ought not to stay here after your drive. You will take cold," said Miss Saville.

"Never you mind," retorted the boy, in a shrill, resentful voice. "I want to speak to Colonel Wilton."

"To me?" said Wilton, coming forward.

"Yes, I have asked them all to bring you to see me, and they won't. I believe they'd like to smother me altogether. Will you come and see me and Ella? I want to hear about a battle and lots of things."

He spoke with a sort of querulous impetuosity.

"I shall be most happy to rub up my recollections for your benefit," said Wilton, good-humoredly, and taking the hand which the little cripple contrived to hold out to him.

"When will you come? To-morrow?"

"I am afraid I cannot," replied Wilton, remembering an engagement with Moncrief, and speaking with very genuine regret.

"Well, the day after?"

"Oh, don't tease, Donny," cried Gertrude Saville.

"The first time Colonel Wilton comes over to

luncheon I will ask him to come and talk to you," said Helen.

"Colonel Wilton, will you just ask for me—Master Fergusson! In the old times, I would be 'Master of Brosedale.'. I shall never see you if you do not."

"Depend on my calling on you," returned Wilton, smiling.

"And soon?"

"Yes, very soon."

Without another word, the unfortunate heir of so much wealth turned and limped into the hall with surprising rapidity.

"How annoying!" cried Gertrude.

"What an awful bore!" said Helen. "Really, Colonel Wilton, I am quite vexed that he should intrude himself upon you."

"Why! I do not see anything vexatious in it."

"You are too good. Do you know that boy is the bane of our existence?"

"Do you wish me to shoot him?" asked Wilton, laughing. "I really cannot wait to do so at present, so good morning, though closing shades almost compel me to say good night."

It was nearly a week before Wilton permitted himself to accept the invitation given him by the heir of Brosedale, and, in the interim, he dined at D——

Castle. The Ladies Mowbray were pleasant, unaffected girls, considerably less imposing and more simple than Helen Saville.

"These are exactly the style of women to please Lord St. George," thought Wilton, as he walked over to Brosedale a day or two after. "And very much the style to please myself formerly; but at present—no. I am wonderfully absorbed by this temporary insanity, which must not lead me too far." Musing in this strain, he reached the grand, brand-new house, where Lady Fergusson and her daughters received him in rich silk morning costumes, very becoming and tasteful, but, somehow, not so pleasant to his eye as the pretty, fresh print dresses of Lord D——'s daughters.

Sir Peter came in to luncheon, which he did not always. His presence generally produced a depressing effect upon his fair step-daughters, and Wilton began to fear that no one would give him an opening to fulfil his promise to the crippled boy. At last he took the initiative himself; and, when Sir Peter paused in an exposition of the opium-trade, Wilton addressed Helen:

"You must not let me break my promise to your brother—step-brother, I mean."

"How! what!" exclaimed Sir Peter to his wife.

"Has he seen Donald?" He spoke in a sharp, startled tone.

"The young gentleman introduced himself to me at the entrance of your hospitable mansion the other day, and expressed a wish to hear my warlike experiences, so I promised to give him a *séance*."

"You are very good," said Sir Peter, slowly, looking down. "Donald has but few pleasures, poor fellow!"

After this, all the talk died out of the little baronet, and he soon rose and left the room.

"Indeed!" cried Gertrude, as the door closed on her step-father, "Donald has tormented us ever since to know when you were coming to see him. You had better take Colonel Wilton to the school-room, Helen, and have done with it."

"I am quite ashamed of troubling you, Colonel Wilton," said Lady Fergusson. "But that boy's whims are very absurd, and Sir Peter is very weak, I must say."

"However, we have had quite a respite since little Miss Rivers came down," interrupted Helen Saville. "She manages him wonderfully. You cannot think what a curious pair they are together. You have seen Donald; and Miss Rivers, though not absolutely plain, is a cold, colorless little thing, generally very silent."

"But she can tell stories delightfully," cried Isabella; "she makes Donald laugh and be quite good-humored for hours together."

"I fear," interrupted the accomplished Miss Walker, "that, if my young charge is too much with Master Fergusson and his companion, her mind will be quite occupied with a very useless array of fairy tales and legends, more calculated to distort than to illustrate historic truth."

"I am sure you are right, Miss Walker. Isabella, you must not go into Donald's room without Miss Walker's permission," remarked Lady Fergusson.

"And she will never let me," said Isabella, with a very rebellious pout.

"Well, well, let us get this visit over," cried Helen, rising. "I will see if he is in the house and visible."

"You cannot think what a nuisance that poor boy was to my girls at first, and how well they bore with him, particularly Helen," said Lady Fergusson. "I am sure Miss Walker did the state great service when she found little Miss Rivers. She suits Donald wonderfully, though she is an oddity in her own way also."

Miss Walker murmured something about "being happy," but her tone was melancholy and uncertain, as though she thought the introduction of an element at variance with historic truth was a doubtful good.

Wilton made no direct reply; he was curious to

ascertain if Miss Rivers had mentioned him, and anxious in any case to play into her hands.

Helen Saville returned quickly.

" Yes," she said, " Donald is at home, and will be highly pleased to see you."

Wilton accordingly followed her through various well-warmed and carpeted passages to a handsome room on the sunny side of the house, which was the dwelling-place of the heir. Books and music, a piano, drawing-materials, globes, pictures, maps, all appliances for amusement and study, gave a pleasant aspect to the apartment. The boy was seated in a chair of elaborate make, furnished with a desk and candle-holder, and which could be raised or lowered to any angle. His crutch lay at hand, and he seemed engaged in drawing. He was plain and unattractive enough—a shrivelled-looking frame, a large head, wide mouth, projecting brow—all the characteristics of deformity. Even large and glittering eyes did not redeem the pale, wan face, over which gleamed a malign expression by no means pleasant to a stranger.

" I thought you would never come," he exclaimed, bluntly, in a harsh, querulous voice, and holding out his hand.

"You will accept me now I am here, I hope," said Wilton, smiling.

" Oh, yes; I am very glad to see you."

"You are an artist, I see?"

"I hope to be one. Look here."

Wilton approached his desk. A sketch lay upon it. A confused mass of figures, apparently intended for a desperate battle.

"This," continued Donald, "is what I wanted you for. This is a study for a large picture in oils (I will begin it when I am a little stronger) of the battle of Balaklava. Nothing has ever been made of this subject, and I want to make something of it; so I thought you would just look at my sketch and see if I have caught an idea of the scene, and correct any inaccuracy that strikes you."

"I should be most happy to help you," returned Wilton, looking hopelessly at the crowd of forms before him; "but I fear my capabilities are not quite equal to the task. In the first place, I was not in the Balaklava affair, and then one's recollections of a battle are not very clear."

"If confusion is a true likeness, Donny's picture will be remarkably successful," said Miss Saville, with a grave manner. Her words brought a flush to the boy's pale brow.

"I wish you would go away," he said, rudely and abruptly. "I can never talk about anything when you are by."

"To hear is to obey," replied Miss Saville, rising;

"only do not try Colonel Wilton's patience too much."

"Go! go!" returned Donald, almost fiercely.

Wilton could not refrain from smiling as she left the room.

"I hate those Savilles!" cried Donald, observing it; "and so would you if you lived in the house with them."

"That is a subject on which we shall never agree. Let us return to your picture," said Wilton, thinking what a thorough "sell" it would be if Ella Rivers never made her appearance; for, with all his surface easy good-nature, Wilton did not fancy sacrificing even a small share of his time to an ill-natured imp like this.

"Look here! I have made this hussar grasp a lancer by the throat, and thrust a sword into his side. Will that do?"

"I see. Well, hardly. You know both hussars and lancers were our men, therefore you must not make them fight; and here you have not the Russian uniform quite correctly. I think I have some sketches of the Russians that would help you. But is it not rather ambitious for such a youngster as yourself to aim at historical painting?"

"That is what Ella says; but it is my only chance of fame." The word on his lips was suggestive of

sadness, and Wilton looked at the frail form, the
pallid face, the thin, tremulous, feverish fingers with
compassion. Before he could reply, a door behind
him opened softly. "Oh, come here, Ella!" cried
Donald. Wilton turned quickly, and just caught a
glimpse of a gray skirt vanishing. "Ella, come
back! Ella! Ella!" screamed the boy, with a sort
of angry impatience that would not be denied.

"I am here, then," she said, reopening the door
and coming in.

Wilton felt his (not inexperienced) heart throb as
she approached, her cheek warm with a soft, flitting
blush, a slight smile upon her lips, but her large eyes
grave and calm. It was the first time Wilton had
seen her in-doors, and the delicate dignity of her look,
especially the setting on of her head, charmed him.
The excessive simplicity of her perpetual gray dress
could not hide the grace of her slim, round form, and
yet he could well imagine that the vulgar, common
taste that looks for rich color and striking outline
might consider the quiet moonlight beauty of this
obscure girl something almost plain.

Wilton greeted her silently as she approached,
with a profound bow. She acknowledged him.

"I did not know you had any one with you," she
said to her pupil.

"Do you know Colonel Wilton?" he asked, sharply.

"He was in the train with me when the collision occurred," she replied quietly, the color fading away from her cheek, and leaving it very pale

"Why did you not tell me?"

"There was nothing to tell, and you never asked me about my adventures."

"This young gentleman is very ambitious," said Wilton, to change the subject. "He is designing to immortalize himself and the Six Hundred at once."

"He will not have patience. I tell him that even the greatest genius must wait and work." She sighed as she spoke. "Besides, it is almost desecration for art to bestow itself on such a subject."

"There!" cried the boy, passionately, "you always discourage me; you are cruel! Have I so much pleasure or hope that you should take this from me?"

She rose from the seat she had taken and came to him, laying her hand on his shoulder with a wonderfully tender gesture. "I do not discourage you, *caro!* You have much ability, but you have scarcely fourteen years. Twenty years hence you will still be young, quite young enough to paint men tearing each other to pieces with immense success. Now, you must learn to walk before you can fly upon the wings of fame. Let us put this away."

6

"No, you shall not. As to twenty years hence, do not talk of them to me!"

The fierce, complaining tone passed from his voice, and he leaned back, raising his eyes to hers with a yearning, loving, sad expression that struck Wilton with strange jealousy. The boy was old for his years, and perhaps, unknown to himself, loved his gentle companion with more than brotherly love. The idea chafed him, and to banish it he spoke :

"Why not make separate studies for your figures? It will practise your hand and make material for your picture. I will send you over the Russian views and figures I have ; they will help you as to costume and scenery."

There was a pause. Wilton was determined not to go away ; and Donald, the fire gone from his eyes, his very figure limp, would not speak. At last, Miss Rivers, who was arranging a box of colors, said, "This gentleman—Colonel Wilton's suggestion is very good. Suppose you act upon it ? And perhaps he will come again, and see how you go on." •

She looked at Colonel Wilton as she spoke, and he tried to make out whether she wished him to return, or to give him the opportunity of escape. Although not inclined to under-estimate himself, he came to the latter conclusion ; but did not avail himself of it.

" You have something more to show me, have you not ! " he asked, kindly.

" Yes ; plenty much better," answered Ella Rivers for him ; and, slipping away the fatal battle-scene, she replaced it with a portfolio full of sketches very unequal in merit. Ella quickly picked out the best, and Donald appeared to cheer up under the encouragement of Wilton's praise.

" Show your sketch of ' Dandy,' " said the boy to Ella.—" She draws very well.—Bring your portfolio, Ella," he went on.

" It is not necessary. You are keeping Colonel Wilton."

" You are not, indeed. I rather fancy you wish to get rid of me, Miss Rivers."

" Miss Rivers ! Miss Rivers ! How did you know her name ? "

" I ? Oh, I have heard it several times ! Your sister mentioned Miss Rivers to-day at luncheon."

" Show your book, Ella, at all events."

She went to a distant table, after a full, searching look at Colonel Wilton, and brought the book he well remembered.

" Here is a capital likeness of my pony and my father's pet Skye. But, Ella, you have torn out a page —the first one. Why ? "

" Because it pleased me to do so." She spoke

very composedly, but the color went and came faintly in her cheek.

"Do tell me why, Ella?" with sharp, angry entreaty.

"I will *not*, Donald! You are tyrannical."

His eyes flashed, but he controlled himself.

"Is not this capital?" he asked, holding out the book.

"Very good—first-rate," returned Wilton, looking at two admirably drawn figures of a pony and dog.

"It is better. I want to improve in animals," said Ella, looking down upon the page; and a little conversation ensued respecting this line of art, in which Donald took no share. Suddenly Ella looked at him. "You are ill! you are suffering!" she exclaimed, darting to his side, and putting her arm round his neck, while, pale as death and half fainting, he rested his head against her breast.

"Pray bring me that phial and glass from the cabinet," she said, quickly. Wilton obeyed; he held the glass while she poured out the right quantity; he took the bottle again, while she held the glass to the poor boy's lips; he assisted to lower the wonderful chair till the weary head could be gently placed in a restful position, all without a word being exchanged; then Ella took the poor, thin hand in hers, and felt the pulse, and stroked it.

Donald opened his eyes. " Ella, I am better ; ask him to say nothing about it."

" I will, dear Donald, I will."—Then, turning to Wilton, " Come, I will show the way." The moment they crossed the threshold she exclaimed, " It will be better to say nothing about it ; Lady Fergusson would only come and make a fuss and torment him, so I troubled you instead of ringing ; but I do not apologize. You would willingly help him, I am sure."

" Yes, of course ; but what a responsibility for you ! "

" Oh, I understand him, and I often see the doctor. Ah, what a life ! what suffering ! what a terrible nature ! But I must not stay. You, you were prudent—that is—pooh ! I am foolish. I mean to say, I am glad you scarcely appeared to know me. I say nothing of myself here ; I am an abstraction, a machine, a companion ! Good-by." For the first time she held out her hand with a gracious, queenly gesture. Wilton took and held it.

" One moment," he said, quickly. " Shall I never have another chance of a word with you in the free air ? Is there no errand to Monkscleugh that may lead to a rencontre ? "

" If I meet you," she said, " I will speak to you ; but it is, and must be, a mere chance. Follow that corridor, turn to the left, and you will be in the hall. Good-by." She was gone.

"Well, what sort of fellow is this cousin of yours? I suppose you met him last night? I never thought we should tumble into the trammels of polite society when I recommended these shootings to you. I have scarcely seen you the last ten days. What's come to you, lad?"

So growled Moncrief one morning as he smoked the after-breakfast cigar, previous to turning out for a run with the "Friarshire."

"Oh! St. George Wilton is rather an amusing fellow; he is tolerably good-looking, and has lots of small talk; one of those men who do not believe much in anything, I fancy, except self and self-interest, but for dear self-sake not disposed to rub other people the wrong way. He is a favorite with the ladies— cuts me out with the fair Helen."

"Hum! I doubt that. I do not think you would let him if he tried; for of course *that's* the attraction to Brosedale."

"Is it?" returned Wilton, carelessly, as he prepared a cigar.

"Yes; I know you think I am as blind as a mole, but I can see there is something that takes you to Brosedale. It's not Sir Peter, though he's the best

of the lot. It's not my lady; and it cannot be that
imp of a boy you are so fond of carrying pictures to—
I suppose for a 'ploy to get into the interior, though
they are sweet enough upon you without that; so it
must be that girl."

"Your reasoning is so admirable," returned Wilton,
laughing good-humoredly, "that I should like to hear
a little more."

"Eh!" said the major, looking up at him curiously.
"Well, my lad, I am only anxious for your own sake.
Helen Saville is not the style of woman Lord St.
George would like; the family are by no means *sans
reproche;* and—I don't fancy her myself."

"That is conclusive," replied Wilton, gravely.
"But make your mind easy; I am not going to marry
Helen Saville, nor do I think she expects me to
do so."

"What she expects, God knows, but there is something not all square about you, Wilton."

"My dear fellow, do you want me to call you
out?"

"You must just go your own way, which, no doubt,
you would in any case; but I am off on Monday next
to pay my sister a visit. I have put her off from time
to time, but I must go now."

"By Jove, I shall be quite desolate! And will
you not return, old fellow?"

"I think not.   At any rate, I shall not be able to come north again till near Christmas ; and I hardly suppose you will be here then."

"That depends," said Wilton, thoughtfully.

"On what ? " asked the major, quickly.

"Oh ! the sport—my own whims—the general attractions of the neighborhood."

" "—— the attractions of the neighborhood ! " cried Moncrief, profanely.   " Why do you not make up to Lady Mary or Lady Susan Mowbray?   They are nice girls and no mistake ; just the very thing for you. But I am a fool to trouble myself about you ; only I have always looked after you since you joined.   However, you are old enough to take care of yourself."

"Perhaps I ought to be, at any rate ; and although I have somehow managed to 'rile' you, I have never forgotten, and never will forget, what a brick you have always been."

Major Moncrief growled out some indistinct words, and went to the window; Wilton followed him. "You'll scarcely manage a run to-day ;" he said ; "the ground is very hard, and, if I am not much mistaken, there's a lot of snow up there," pointing to a dense mass of heavy drab clouds to windward.

"No," returned Moncrief, uncertainly, "it is considerably milder this morning; besides, the wind is too high, and it is too early for snow."

" Not in these latitudes ; and it has been deucedly
cold for the week past."

" At any rate, I will go to the meet," said Moncrief,
leaving the room. " What are you going to do ? "

" I shall not hunt to-day ; I am going over to
Monkscleugh."

" Hum ! to buy toys for the child ? "

" Yes," said Wilton, laughing. " But for to-day I
am safe : Lady Fergusson and her fair daughter,
attended by our diplomatic cousin, are going to
Brantwood, where there is a coming-of-age ball, or
some such high-jinks. They politely invited me to be
of the party ; but I resisted, Moncrief—I resisted ! "

" Did you, by George ! That puzzles me."

" By St. George, you mean. Why, you suspicious
old boy, you do seem not satisfied ; and yet Helen
Saville will be away three or four days."

" I'll be hanged if I can make you out ! " said the
major, and walked away.

Wilton threw himself into an arm-chair and laughed
aloud ; then he turned very grave, and thought long
and deeply. If Moncrief only knew where the real
danger lay, and what it was ! How was it that he had
permitted this mere whim, half curiosity, half compassion, to grow into such troublesome proportions ?
He knew it was folly, and yet he could not resist !
He had always felt interested and attracted by that

strange girl whose mingled coldness and sweetness charmed and wounded him ; but now, since he had seen her oftener, and listened to her voice, and heard the sudden but rare outbreaks of enthusiasm and feeling which would force themselves into expression, as if in spite of her will, he was conscious that his feelings were deepening into intense passion and tenderness.

To catch a sympathetic look, a special smile, a little word to himself alone—such were the nothings watched for, sought, treasured, remembered by our patrician soldier. The vision of that poor, suffering boy leaning his head against Ella and clasped in her arms, seemed indelibly stamped upon his brain. It was constantly before him, though he fought gallantly against it.

It seemed to have brought about a crisis of feeling. Before that, though touched, interested, curious, he was not absorbed ; now, reason as he would, resist as he would, he could not banish the desperate longing to be in that boy's place just for once. In short, Wilton was possessed by one of those rare but real passions which, when they seize upon a man of his age, are infinitely more powerful, more dangerous, or, as the case may be, more noble, than when they partake of the eager effervescence of youth.

And what was to be the end thereof ?—so he asked

himself as, starting from his seat, he paced the room.

Ardently as he felt, he could not but acknowledge that to marry a girl, not only in a position little more than menial, but of whose antecedents he knew absolutely nothing—who, for some mysterious reason, did not seem to have a friend on earth—was a piece of folly he ought to be ashamed to commit. And yet to give her up—worse still, to leave her for some demure curate, some enterprising bagman to win, perhaps to trample upon? Impossible!

What then? It must not be asserted that the possibility of some tie less galling and oppressive than matrimony never presented itself to Ralph Wilton's mind. He had known such conditions among his friends, and some (according to his lax but not altogether unpopular opinions) had not turned out so badly for any of the parties concerned ; but in this case he rejected the idea as simply out of the question. He would no more dare breathe it to that obscure little girl than to a princess. It would be hard enough to win or rouse her to admit him as a lover, even on the most honorable terms. She seemed not to think such things existed for her. There was in her such a curious mixture of frankness and indifference, coldness, sweetness, all flecked with sparks of occasional fire, that Wilton could not help believing she had some uncommon history; and there were times when he felt that, if he but asked her, she would tell him everything he craved to know. Never had he met a woman (for, young as she was, she was eminently womanly) so utterly without coquetry. Her perfect freedom from this feminine ingredient was almost insulting, and a certain instinct warned him from attempting to break through the invisible barrier which her unconscious simplicity created. Yet all this restraint was becoming intolerable. At Brosedale he never saw her alone; out of it, he never saw her at all. The desire to know all about her, to impress her, to win her, and the struggling instinct of caste, the dread of making some false step that would ruin him in her estimation, tormented him almost into a fever.

His long meditation ended in his ringing sharply, and ordering round the dog-cart to drive into Monks-cleugh.

"It's sure to snow, sir," said his servant.

"Not yet, I think. At any rate, I shall take my chance."

"Yes," he continued, half aloud, as the man disappeared, "I must make the attempt; and if I meet her—why, what will be, will be!" With this profoundly philosophic conclusion he proceeded to draw on an overcoat and prepare for his cold drive.

The previous day, Wilton had managed, by a profound stratagem, to procure an interview with Donald, and for his pains found that young gentleman fearfully cross and rude, moreover alone : but, in the course of their short conversation, the heir of Brosedale confessed to being greatly enraged at the non-appearance of some fresh drawing-materials which had been forwarded from London, and of which no tidings could be heard ; that " Dandy," his special pony, was ill or disabled, and no one was at liberty to go for them ; so Ella had promised to walk over to Monkscleugh the next morning.

Of course Wilton discovered that he, too, had " urgent private affairs " of his own to transact in the town, and, had it " rained elephants and rhinoceroses," he would have persevered.

It was a still, cold morning. The bitter wind of the day before had fallen, and a kind of expectant hush pervaded the air. The man who stood at the horse's head, looked round him with a very dissatisfied air, not seeing the necessity for driving to Monkscleugh.

However, the drive there was accomplished without any encounter, save with a barefooted lassie on her way to market. At first Wilton drove slowly, and then fast, and before they had reached the town the snow had begun, in large, slow flakes. In spite of its increasing density, he managed to call at the saddler's and the corn-factor's, and twice at the railway-station, but all in vain ; so, with a muttered malediction on the weather, which had, no doubt, defeated the object of his expedition, he turned his horse's head toward home.

" It's going to be a bad fall," he said to his servant, as they proceeded through the thickly-descending snow, which scarcely permitted them to see a yard right or left.

" It is so, sir ; and I wish we were home, or, any-how, across the brae there, where the road turns to Brosedale."

" Do you think we will lose the track ? "

" I'll be surprised if we do not, sir."

" I fancy I shall be able to make it out," returned Wilton, and drove on as rapidly as he could in silence. Suddenly he pulled up. " Look," said he, " there— to the right. Do you not see something like a figure —a woman ? "

" Faith, it's only a big stone, sir ! "

" No—it moves !—Hallo ! " shouted Wilton. " I think you are off the road."

The figure stopped, turned, and came toward them. Wilton immediately sprang down and darted forward, exclaiming, " Miss Rivers ! Good God ! what weather for you ! How fortunate I overtook you.—Come, let me assist you to reach my dog-cart. You must be nearly wet through."

She put her hand on his offered arm. "It is indeed fortunate you came up. I had begun to feel bewildered." Nevertheless she spoke quite calmly, and accepted his aid to mount the dog-cart with perfect composure. As Wilton took his place beside her and gathered up the reins, after wrapping his plaid round her, he made up his mind very rapidly not to attempt the longer and more open route to Brosedale.

He drove more slowly, taking good heed of the objects he could make out, and, to his great joy, recognized a certain stunted, gnarled oak, to the right of which lay Glenraven, and, having passed it, somewhat increased his speed.

"It is scarcely wise to push on to Brosedale until this heavy fall is over. Besides, the Lodge is much nearer, and you ought not to be a moment longer than you can help in these wet clothes. I am afraid you must depend on the resources of our cook for dry garments."

"My clothes are not so very wet, but my boots are. I wish we could have gone on to Brosedale ; but, if it cannot be, I will not trouble you. This snow is too heavy to last very long."

"Pray Heaven it may !" said Wilton inwardly.

Here was the first gleam of good fortune that had visited him. Ella was to be all alone with him for two or three hours. Snow or no snow, he would manage that, at all events. All the Brosedale women away, Moncrief certain to be storm-stayed somewhere —what a glorious chance for a long, confidential talk, for the solving of many doubts, for the forging of some link that would bind this wild, free bird to him! The excessive delight and exaltation that made his heart bound roused him to the necessity of self-control, and he swore to himself that not a word or a look should escape him to offend or startle his prize.

" How was it you ventured out on so unpromising a morning?" he asked, as they proceeded, stopping from time to time to make sure of the road.

" Oh, Donald was so ravenous to get a parcel which he thought must be mislaid at Monkscleugh, that I promised to go over for it; and you know I love so much to be out. Still I do not think I should have attempted it, only a Mr. Wilton, who was going somewhere in the phaeton, offered to drive me to Monkscleugh. I thought it would snow, but I hoped to get back before it began. However, I was overtaken; and I fancy I should have wandered all day had you not found me."

" I thought Wilton was going with Lady Fergusson to the *fête* at Brantwood?"

" He was; but he was to take up some one on the way."

" He is a relation of mine," said Wilton, feeling

marvellously crossed by the simple fact of St. George having discovered the hidden treasure as well as himself.

" I suppose so ; but he is quite unlike you."

It would be hard to say, logically, why this comforted Colonel Wilton, but it did.

" Hold hard, sir !" cried the groom, who was standing up and peering ahead. " You will be right against the gate." And Wilton found he was at home. Another moment and he pulled up at the door of the Lodge.

CHAPTER V.

"SEND Mrs. McKollop here," cried Wilton, hastily and imperiously, to Major Moncrief's servant, who advanced to the door. "One of the Brosedale ladies has been caught in the snow, and is nearly wet through."

He almost lifted Ella from the dog-cart as he spoke, and led her into the warm, comfortable hall. While he removed the plaid that wrapped his guest, the astonished Mrs. McKollop came quickly on the scene.

"Eh, my word! but ye're wet!" she exclaimed "Come wi' me, missee, and I'll see till ye; and you'd be the better of a drop of hot toddy yerse'f, colonel."

"Oh, I shall be all right! Just look to Miss Rivers.—As soon as you have got rid of your wet things we will have luncheon," he added, addressing her. She bowed, and followed the portly Mrs. McKollop.

"I hope there is some place fit to take a lady into," said Wilton to Major Moncrief's man, on whom the domestic arrangements devolved, for he was barely acquainted with Mrs. McKollop's name. This important functionary was attached to Glenraven Lodge, and let with the premises. To this species of serfdom she was by no means averse, for the system proved profitable, and, by a sort of mental inversion, she had grown to regard the temporary proprietors as her guests and vassals.

"Yes, sir, I believe Mrs. McKollop keeps the top rooms pretty tidy."

"Well, get luncheon, will you? I hope the fire is good." So saying, Wilton hastened to change his own damp clothes, and don a black velvet shooting-jacket. His toilet was completed, and he was fully a quarter of an hour in the dining-room before any one appeared. "Go and let Miss Rivers know luncheon is ready." A few minutes more, and the door opened to admit his guest. An expression of demure fun sparkled in her eyes as she came in, holding up the voluminous drapery of Mrs. McKollop's best dress—a strongly-pronounced Mac-something tartan, of bright red and green and yellow—which was evidently a world too wide for her slight waist. Above was the close-fitting gray jacket of her own dress, which had been saved from wet by her water-proof.

"I trust you have been made tolerably comfortable?" said Wilton, placing a chair for her, while he glanced with much satisfaction at the fast falling snow.

"Your house-keeper has been so good," she replied, with her sweetest, frankest smile. "She exhausted all her resources to supply my wants, and, I think, would fain have made me come to luncheon in her best bonnet, which is the most wonderful thing you ever saw. It has feathers, and flowers, and currants in it."

"I suppose carrots and turnips would be too much like the insignia of office. But you must be exhausted. Pray sit down and have some luncheon."

"Thank you. I do feel rather hungry."

It seemed almost incredible to be sitting *tête-à-tête* with Ella, after all his dreams and efforts ; but even more surprising was her quiet, unembarrassed manner. Had Wilton been her grandfather, she could not have eaten with more composure, and, it must be added, zest, showing a decided preference for cold game and sweets.

"Let me recommend some hot wine-and-water," said Wilton, as she put down her knife and fork, after refusing a second supply of grouse.

"Thank you, no. I never take wine ; but, if I might ask for something ? "

"Certainly ; anything within the resources of Glenraven and Mrs. McKollop."

"Then may I have a cup of coffee ? "

Wilton immediately ordered it ; and, when it came, his guest expressed high approval.

"Ah! your people have learned how to make this in France."

"From Frenchmen, at any rate. That was one accomplishment our servants picked up."

"The coffee at Brosedale is so dead ; it is not the least like coffee! This reminds me of Italy and France."

"Then you have been a good deal abroad?"

"Nearly all my life." A full stop ; and Wilton felt he had led up neatly to the story of her past.

"As you will take nothing more, suppose we go into the next room?" She rose, and then stopped.

"Oh! I have lost Mrs. McKollop's shoe under the table." Wilton laughed, and assisted in the search.

"I wish we had anything nearer the mark to offer you," he said, as he produced a huge, broad-soled thick shoe, tied on the instep. "They must fit you like snow-shoes."

"There is a good deal of stocking to fill up with," she replied, as she managed to shuffle into the room on the opposite side of the hall, which was somewhat more ornamental than the one they left. Sundry sporting prints, a deer's head, various pipes, and plenty of writing-materials, with a splendid fire, and several comfortable easy-chairs, made it a pleasant apartment.

"And you live here?" said Ella Rivers, moving round the room with some curiosity; "and you smoke very good cigars. I recognize the perfume."

"I hope it is not very disagreeable?"

"Disagreeable? Oh, no! I love it. But how it snows! There is no chance of my getting back till it abates."

"Certainly not," returned Wilton, cheerfully, and adopting her easy, friendly tone. "So, pray sit down near the fire, and permit me to enjoy the fruit of my treasure-trove—I mean, a little talk with you."

"Yes—it is very nice to talk over a good fire," she said, returning slowly from the window and seating herself in a large chair; "but I wish it would clear."

"I suppose young Fergusson will be very anxious about you?" remarked Wilton, taking advantage of her steady gaze at the fire to study the graceful outline of her head, and ear, and neck, the pale, delicate oval of her face. There was a wonderfully-patrician look about this mysterious girl; how small and white were the hands she had carelessly clasped upon her knee! and, simple as were her manners, too, they were infinitely more refined than the superb Miss Saville's; and, at all events, he would have her all to himself for the next two hours.

"Anxious about me?" she said, after a moment's silence; "not very. He will be anxious about his parcel (which, after all, I did not get), and vexed at my absence. But Donald is a strange boy. I know him."

"He must be an ungrateful young dog," said Wilton, carefully averting his eyes as she turned to him. "You are so good to him."

"It is not what you would call grateful, though he is very fond of me—that is, I have become a necessity to him; then he knows I am fond of him, and I believe no one else is, not even his father. Poor, poor fellow! Ah, how I feel for him!"

"He cannot be a pleasant companion."

"At times most unpleasant; then, again, wonderfully sympathetic, and so dependent that *I* feel a great, strong, free creature, rich in youth, and health, and strength, all grand things that Sir Peter's gold cannot buy, and I can do anything for him. Then I forget the dark side of my own lot, and only see the wealth that nature has given me."

"You are, indeed, wealthy!"

"In some ways, yes; in others—" She stopped, shook her head, with a smile, half-sad, half-mocking, and resumed her gaze at the fire.

There was a short pause, and Wilton said:

"Still, to so bold a spirit as yours, it must be im-

prisonment, indeed ; and I am not surprised that you
seize every chance of momentary relief. But—forgive
me if I am presumptuous—it was no ordinary courage
that would take you so far afield that night I caught
a glimpse of you retreating in the moonlight—no
ordinary inducement that would tempt you to such a
distance."

"I had inducement enough," she returned, with a
slight sigh. "Donald had been in one of his worst
moods all day—one of his mean, suspicious tempers,
and I could not persuade him to go to bed till late.
Then, I opened the study window, and looked out to
breathe and grow tranquil before I tried to sleep
then the memory of the moonlight nights long ago,
when I used to sit in a corner by the window, before
the lamp was brought, and listen to my father talking
(rather dreaming aloud—oh, so gloriously !) came
over me with a wild, irresistible longing to be out in
the free air, alone and standing upright before heaven,
with things *really* greater than myself about me—*such*
an intense longing that I sprang down the steps and
away." As she said the last word she unclasped her
h nds and threw one out with a sudden, expressive
gesture full of grace, and not without a certain dignity. "But I suppose to you it seems shocking ?"
And again she turned to the fire.

"By no means!" exclaimed Wilton, eagerly.

"Pray do not imagine me a slave to 'the shocking.'
What you do seems right and natural in you to an
extraordinary degree ; but every one may not view
matters as I do, and I confess I wished to escort you
back, but dared not intrude—besides, I was not
alone."

"Escort me back ! " she replied, with a low, sweet
laugh of genuine merriment. " That would have put
a climax to my misdoings, and also (pardon the
rudeness destroyed the sense of freedom. As it was,
my outbreak was severely rebuked by Miss Walker,
who was informed of my absence, and talked yards
of sense and propriety before I escaped to bed. Ah,
what a degrading *finale* to a moment's outbreak into
light and liberty ! But I must not quarrel with Miss
Walker. She is 'Madonna dell' Esperanza.'"

There was a wonderful charm in her voice and
manner, a curious mixture of softness and daring.

" And pray why do you dignify that iron-gray
woman with so romantic a title ? I should not imagine her in the least hopeful."

" She found me when I was at a very low ebb, and
placed me with Donald."

" Indeed ! Then he ought to consider her his
' Dame de bon Secours.'"

" He thinks I am fortunate."

" And, when you found yourself so far from human

aid that night, did you not feel uncomfortable?" resumed Wilton, hoping to lead her back to her reminiscences.

"Yes. When I turned to go back the fire had
nearly burnt out in my heart ; but, you see, I have
never been with women, so their fears are not mine.
I fear what they may think of me when I act differently from them."

"I suppose, then, you have numerous brothers?"

"I have neither brother nor sister. My father—"
She paused. "Ah, if you could have known my
father! He was a great politician, a great philan-
thropist, a true man ; and he was surrounded by men
like himself, devoted to humanity. They were all
very good to me—when they remembered my existence, which was not always, you know." A little
arch smile, that made Wilton burn to tell her how
irresistibly she absorbed his mind, heart, imagination!

"Well, your father," said he, with wonderful composure, rising as he spoke to arrange the fire—"your
father, I presume, adored you?"

"Alas, no!" There was great forgiving tenderness in her voice. "He perhaps remembered me
least of all ; and when he did, I brought bitter
thoughts. My mother, whom he adored, died when I
was born ; so you see I have been quite alone. Yet I

grew to be of importance to him; for just before he died he told me to take her ring, which he had always worn, and wear it for both their sakes. See, there it is."

She held out her right hand to show where it encircled her slender third finger.

"Then you lived in Italy?" said Wilton, to lead her on.

"Yes, my first memories are of Italy—a great, half-ruined villa on a hill-side near Genoa; and my nurse, a Roman woman, with such grand, black eyes. I used to love to look into them, and see myself in them. How she loved me and spoiled me! My father must have had money then, for he came and went, and seemed to me a great·person; but I feared him, though he was gentle and beautiful, for he shunned me. Oh, yes, how noble he looked! None of the others were like him; and he was English on his father's side, so he said, when he told me to keep the name of Rivers; but we had many names: one in Italy, another in Paris, another in Germany. I did not like Paris. The first time we were there I had a *gouvernante;* she taught me a little and tormented me much; but still I do know French best. I can write it well; but, though I speak Italian and German, I cannot read or write either."

She had again clasped her hands over her knee,

and went on softly and dreamingly, as if to herself.
Wilton still keeping silence, and gazing intently at the
speaker, earnestly hoping nothing would interrupt or
turn her from her spoken musing.

"But you evidently learned to draw," he suggested,
softly.

"My father was a great artist—would have been
acknowledged as a great artist had he not been gradually absorbed in schemes for raising the poor and
ignorant and oppressed, for giving them political life.
There were many artists among our friends, and
all were willing to teach me and help me. To draw
seemed to me as natural as to breathe, and if I ever
had a moment of personal ambition it was to be a
true, a recognized artist; but I had scarcely any.
You, even you, patrician Englishman as you are!"
turning to him with sudden animation, "you would
have admired my father. He was my ideal of a true
knight, so simple, so noble, so refined; with such a
deep, fervent faith in his fellow-men. Of course, he
and all our friends were hunted, proscribed; so I
never knew a relation. And he, my father, never
could bear to speak of my mother; so I only know from
her picture that she was fair and sweet-looking."

"What a strange, sad life for a girl!" said Wilton,
with genuine sympathy.

"Strange, but not sad. Oh, no! I was ignorant

(I am ignorant, by your standard), and not a little neglected. But what delight it was to listen to the men my father knew, to hear the grand schemes they planned; the noble, tender pity for the suffering and oppressed; the real brotherhood they acknowledged to all mankind, and the zest of danger; for often a well-loved comrade was missing, and some never returned. Imprisonment in Italy or Prussia for a political offence is a serious matter.

"The first time I ever won real notice from my father was at Naples. There was a man we loved much; he was called Diego—it was not his real name. He was very much suspected by the government. My father found out he was to be seized that day, and he knew not whom to trust to send him word; so I begged to be honored by his permission to carry the message, and I managed it all. I borrowed a costume from my maid's niece; I went alone on the Corso, and offered bunches of violets to every one—oh! I had heaps of *paoli*—till I met him and said the word, which sufficed."

"You did this?" cried Wilton.

"Yes; I had but thirteen years then. Oh! my father always noticed me after; and I would have dared much for that. Then we were in London, and in many places—we grew poorer and poorer. I think my father helped the cause largely. Two years ago

we were in Paris, and then I saw my father was dying.
There were very few of our clique there, for the empe-
ror's spies were legion. I did not stop to think of
fear or grief; I only wanted to keep him quiet and
content to the last, for, you see"—with a sort of exultation very touching—"I was now very important to
him—he thought more of me, and I have always
believed it was in the hope of arranging some shelter,
some refuge, for me that he came to London, now
more than two years ago. Diego came to see us. He
had a long talk with my father, who said to him, when
he was going, ' Do your best for her sake!'

"Two days after, Diego came again, and demanded
to see my father alone. Presently there was a cry;
they called me, and, when I went in, my father lay in
Diego's arms, the blood streaming from his mouth.
He died two days after." An instant's pause, and
she resumed, quickly: "I was quite alone, and had
but a few shillings. Poor Diego, how good he was!
He did much for me. My father had a diamond ring;
they sold it, and so things were paid for. Diego, poor
fellow! he was rich then—he had five gold-pieces—
sovereigns. He left me two. He was obliged to go
away; he promised Mrs. Kershaw to come back for
me, but he never came. He is no doubt imprisoned
or killed."

"Who was Mrs. Kershaw?" asked Wilton, huskily; "and how old is this Diego?"

"Diego? Oh, fifty—sixty—I am not sure. Mrs. Kershaw is the landlady of the lodgings where my father died; Such a strange woman! Not unkind—at all events, to me. There was a lady in the rooms above ours who was very kind to me, and felt for me; and nearly five months after I was left quite alone. Miss Walker came to stay with this lady, and so they managed to have me engaged as companion to Donald. Ah, it was all so wretched! Nothing reconciled me to Brosedale but the scenery—that made me remember there was a world of life and beauty beyond Donald's study."

She stopped, and leaning back, pressed both hands over her face, as if to shut out the present. Wilton scarce knew how to speak to her without saying too much. He had sufficiently delicate instincts to feel that he must not, when she was in such a mood, show, by the slightest indication, that he was her lover; nay, his deep sympathy made him for the moment forget the fair woman in the lonely, suffering girl.

"And had none of your father's friends a wife or a sister with whom you might have taken shelter? Brosedale, under such circumstances, must have been a real *inferno.*"

"No; I have met one or two ladies abroad con-

nected with our cause, and they were far away.   But
Brosedale was more astonishing than anything else.
Miss Walker, who likes me, although I shock her
every hour in the day, warned me of the respect I
must show to 'miladi' and her daughters, and I never
dreamed of disrespect toward them ; but they were—
they are so strange ; they are so ignorant; they belong
to the middle ages.   When I spoke to them of the
scenery, when I asked them questions about their
country, when I addressed them as my fellow creatures,
they were petrified—they were indignant; they went
through a little comedy of insulted majesty, very droll,
but not pleasant.   Then I began to know what it is
to believe that you are made of different clay from
certain others of your fellows.   Alas! what wide gulfs
still yawn between man and man, and what precious
things must be cast in before they are filled up ! "

"Well, and Donald—how did you get on with
Donald ? "

"He was inclined to treat me like a petted animal; but, no ! *Per Baccho!* that should not be.   I
said, 'If you are good, you shall call me Ella, and I
will call you Donald.'   He replied, 'I am Master
Fergusson ;' and I said, 'Not so—it is too long.
Besides, I am your superior in age and in knowledge,
so between us there shall be kindness and freedom.'
Now I mark my displeasure by calling him Master

Fergusson. Ah! how astonished were Miss Walker and 'miladi,' but I laughed."

" I am surprised he can bear you out of his sight," exclaimed Wilton, warmly, and checked himself; but she only noticed his words.

" He does not like me to be away. I am often imprisoned for weeks. Last August I grew weak and languid; so Lady Fergusson gave me a holiday. I had nowhere to go but to Mrs. Kershaw's ; then she was taken ill—a bad fever—so I nursed her, thankful to be of use. Then Donald summoned me back, and "—turning with the peculiar air of gracious acknowledgment which Wilton had before noticed, she added—" it was on my journey back I met you. Oh, how weary I was! I had been awake night after night. I was stupefied with fatigue, and you were so good. Could Death then have come to me in sleep, I should have held out my arms to him. Yet you see I was terrified at the idea of being hurt or torn when the train was overset."

" You behaved like—like an angel, or rather like a true, high-souled woman."

She laughed softly, and rising, attempted to walk to the window.

" Ah ! " she exclaimed, " I forgot my shoes ; " then, resuming her seat, went on : " There, I have told you all my life. Why, I cannot say ; but, if I have

8

wearied you, it is your own fault. You listened as if you cared to hear, while to me it has been sad, yet sweet, to recall the past, to talk of my father to one who will not mock at his opinions—his dreams, if you will. But, ah! what dreams! what hopes! Thank God! he lived to know of Garibaldi's triumph—to see the papal throne tremble at the upheaval of Italy! These glimpses of light gladdened him at the last; for never was Christian martyr upheld by faith in a future world more steadfastly than my father by his belief in the political regeneration of this one. Yet I have, perhaps, forgotten myself in speaking so much."

She turned toward Wilton as she spoke, and, placing her elbow on the arm of the chair, rested her chin in the palm of her hand, looking at him with the large, deep-blue eyes which had so struck him at first, her long lashes wet with tear drops, of which she was unconscious.

"At least," said Wilton, "you must feel that no speaker ever riveted attention more than you have. As for the accuracy of the opinions so disinterestedly upheld, I neither combat nor assent to them. I can only think of you—so young, so alone?"

It is impossible to say how much passionate sympathy he was about to express, when a sudden change in Ella Rivers's face made him stop and turn round. To his infinite annoyance there stood Major

Moncrief, with the door in his hand, and an expression of utter blank astonishment on his countenance, his coat covered with fast-melting snow, and evidently just dismounted.

" Hallo, Moncrief ! " cried Wilton, his every-day, sharp senses recalled in a moment by this sudden, unwelcome apparition. " Wet to the skin, I suppose, like Miss Rivers "—a wave of the hand toward her— —" and myself. I most fortunately overtook her half-way from Monkscleugh, and brought her here for shelter."

" Oh ! " ejaculated Moncrief: it sounded like a groan.

" You have met my chum, Major Moncrief, have you not, Miss Rivers ? "

She shook her head. " You know I am always with Donald."

" Oh, ah, I see ! " muttered Moncrief. " No, I have never had the pleasure of meeting the young lady before ; and so, Wilton, I will not interrupt you. I will go and change my clothes."

" Interrupt ! " said Ella, as he left the room. " What does he mean by interrupt ? Who is he ?— your uncle—your guardian ? "

" Do you think I require a guardian at my age ? " replied Wilton, laughing, though greatly annoyed at Moncrief's tone.

" How old are you ? " asked Ella, but so softly and simply that the question did not seem rude.

" Almost four and thirty ; and, *en revanche,* how old are you ? "

" Almost twenty."

" I should not have thought you so much : yet there are times you look more. However, Moncrief is an old brother-officer of mine ; really a friend, but a queer fellow, a little odd."

" I see ; and I do not think he likes me to be here. Can I not go ? " said Ella, starting up and making her way to the window, although she left a shoe behind her in her progress.

" Not like you ! More probably fascinated at first sight," returned Wilton, attempting to laugh off the impression she had received, though feeling terribly annoyed at Moncrief's manifestation. " And, as to returning, you cannot stir just yet ; the snow has only just cleared off and may recommence."

" Still I should so much like to return ; and I am sure I could manage to walk very well."

" I do not wish to be oppressively hospitable, so I will leave you for a moment to inquire what will be the best mode of reaching Brosedale."

So saying, he quitted the room and followed Major Moncrief.

He found that excellent soldier in his dressing-gown, and wearing a more "gruesome" expression than could be accounted for by his occupation, viz., sipping some scalding-hot whiskey-and-water.

" Have you had anything to eat ? " asked Wilton, amiably. - " I believe luncheon is still on the table."

" No, it is not," replied the major, curtly ; " and I do not want anything. I had a crust of bread and cheese at that farmer's below the mill, so you can go back to your charming guest."

" And you must come with me, Moncrief. Never mind the dressing-gown, man ; it is quite becoming. You frightened Miss Rivers, you looked so ' dour ' just now. I want her to see what a pleasant fellow you can be."

" Thank you ; I am not quite such a muff as to spoil a *tête-à-tête.*"

" Come, Moncrief, you know that is bosh. I overtook Miss Rivers as she was struggling through the snow, and I do not suppose you or any other man would have left her behind. Then I couldn't possibly pass my own gate in such a storm ; besides, the poor girl was so wet. Be that as it may, you shall not be uncivil ; so finish your grog, and come along."

" Let me put on my coat. If I am to play propriety, I must dress accordingly. How in the name of Fortune did you come to know this Miss Rivers ? " growled Moncrief.

"Why, at Brosedale, of course. Whenever they dragged me in to see that poor boy she was there, and one can't be uncivil to a woman, and a pretty girl to boot."

"Pretty!" ejaculated the major, thrusting himself with unnecessary vehemence into his coat. "I did not see much prettiness about her; she has big eyes, that's all."

"Come and have another look then, and perhaps you will find it out," said Wilton, pleasantly, as sorely against his will Moncrief followed him down stairs.

"I have much pleasure in introducing two such admirable representatives of two great opposing systems. Major Moncrief is conservative among conservatives; Miss Rivers revolutionary among democrats!" said Wilton.

"You say so for me; I myself scarce know enough to be anything," she replied, in a low tone, turning from the window at which she was standing when they entered, acknowledging the introduction and Moncrief's "boo," as he would have called it, by a slight, haughty courtesy, which even Mrs. McKollop's plaid dress did not spoil, as she spoke.

"A young lady confessing ignorance on any subject is a *rara avis* nowadays," returned Moncrief, gloomily.

Ella Rivers looked earnestly at him as he spoke,

and then glanced, with a sort of mute appeal, to Wilton, who felt instinctively that, in spite of her composed, brave air, her heart was beating with sorrowful indignation at the major's unfriendly aspect.

"You must know, Miss Rivers," said Wilton, with his pleasantest smile, longing all the time to fall upon and thrash desperately his good friend and comrade—"you must know that my friend Moncrief is the gloomy ascetic of the regiment, always available for the skeleton's part at the feast, that is, the mess, a terror to lively subs, and only cheerful when some one in a terrible scrape requires his help to get out of it; but one grows accustomed even to a skeleton. I have been shut up with him for nearly six weeks, and, you see, I have not committed suicide yet; but he is a first-rate old Bones after all!" (slapping the ungenial major on the shoulder).

"Is he really unhappy?" asked Ella, with such genuine wonder and curiosity that the "dour" major yielded to the irresistible influences, and burst into a gracious laugh, in which Wilton joined, and the cloud which Moncrief brought with him was almost dispersed—not quite, for Ella was changed pale, composed, silent, with an evidently unconscious drawing to Wilton's side, that did not help to steady his pulse or cool his brain.

"It is quite clear," said Miss Rivers, anxiously;

"may I not return? for in another hour night will close. I must go!"

"Certainly!" cried Wilton, who was feeling dreadfully bored by the flagging conversation and general restraint of Moncrief's presence; "your dress will be dry by this time, and while you put it on I will order the dog-cart. I will drive you over to Brosedale in half an hour, snow or no snow."

"You—drive me—oh, no! I can walk quite well; I am not the least afraid. Do not come out again."

"My dear Miss Rivers! allow you to walk alone? Impossible! Even this stern Bones, this incarnation of inexorable Fate, would not demand such a sacrifice. —Moncrief, ring the bell; summon Mrs. McKollop from the vasty deep to attend our fair guest.—You must know, Miss Rivers, my brother-in-arms is part proprietor of this sylvan lodge."

"Then will he forgive my intrusion," said their guest, with an air so deprecating as to a man of his age, so certainly dignified as to herself, yet so simple withal, that the hidden spring of chivalry far down in the man's nature was struck and pushed to the surface all the more strongly for the depth of the boring.

"You must think me 'a skeleton of the feast,' indeed, as Wilton has been good enough to describe me, if I were not ready to welcome the chance visit of a charming young lady ; I am not quite so hopeless an old ' Bones ' as you both make out."

" Bravo ! " cried Wilton, highly pleased at his change of tone.

" Thank you ! " said Miss Rivers, simply ; and then the door opened to admit Mrs. McKollop, who wore upon her arm a mass of drapery, and in her hand a very small pair of boots, evidently the garments she had been drying.

" They are all nice an' weel aired, if you be going," said the benign ruler of the roost. " It's a wee bit clear just noo, but I'm thinking the frost is coming on, so the snaw will be harder by-an'-by ; an' if the major don't mind having dinner an hour before his usual time, a drap o' hare soup and a cut out of a loin o' mountain mutton will warm ye up weel, an' mak' ye ready for the road," or, as she pronounced it, " rod."

" Mrs. M'Kollop, you are a most sensible woman," said Wilton, gravely. Moncrief looked alarmed ; and Miss Rivers merely observed, " I will come with you," and left the room, accompanied by the friendly cook. Wilton followed immediately, to give orders about the dog-cart, and Major Moncrief was left alone. He walked once or twice up and down the room with a troubled and irate expression ; he then stirred the fire viciously, threw down the poker with a clang, and, drawing a chair close up, thrust his feet almost against the bars. How long he sat in gloomy reverie he knew not, but he was roused by the entrance of Wilton, who ushered in their guest, saying, " Miss Rivers wants to say good-by, Moncrief."

" Yes, good-by ! " said she, in her soft yet clear voice, which always seemed to fix attention. " Thank you—thank you both for your kind hospitality."

With a slight, touching hesitation she held out her hand, and Moncrief took it with much politeness and an altered expression.

" Good-by, then, as you will not stay for the hare soup and a cut of the mountain mutton. I hope you will not take cold. Have you nothing to put round your throat ? You must have this muffler of mine, if you will condescend to wear it.—Jump up, Wilton. I will help Miss Rivers."

So spoke the Major, in his joy to speed the parting guest. Wilton obeyed, somewhat amused, and they started. But the drive was a silent one on Miss Rivers's side ; all Wilton's dexterous observations and thoughtful care could not win a look—scarce a word. " Does she regret she opened her heart to me ? " he thought ; and, as they neared the great house, he could not refrain from saying, " I shall often think of the interesting sketch you have given me of your wan- . derings in many lands, Miss Rivers, though I shall only speak of them to yourself."

"Pray, pray, put it all out of your mind! I am half ashamed of having talked so much of myself. Think no more of it."

"Suppose the subject will not be banished? I cannot. At least," resumed Wilton, after a moment's pause to tighten the reins of his self-control, "I shall look upon liberal politics with a new light, after the glimpse you have given me of their inner life."

"If, when you have power, you will think of the people, I am not sorry I spoke." She said it very softly, almost sadly.

"I shall look in to-morrow, to know if you are all right," he replied.

They had now reached the entrance. Wilton sprang down, and, as Miss Rivers was muffled in plaids, nearly lifted her from the carriage, though with all the deference he would have shown a princess.

"Good-by! I hope you will not be the worse."

"Adieu!" For a moment she raised her eyes to his with a frank, kind glance, and vanished into the house.

For a moment Wilton hesitated, then mounted the dog-cart, and drove back as fast as circumstances would allow. He was conscious of an angry, uncomfortable sensation toward Moncrief—a feeling that it would be a great relief to avoid dining with him—of a curious, uneasy strain of dissatisfaction with himself—with the

routine of life—with everything ! It was so infernally
stupid, smoking and reading, or listening to Moncrief's
prosings, all the evening ; while that cranky, tiresome
boy, Fergusson, would be talked to, and soothed, and
petted by Ella Rivers. And she—would she wish to
be back at Glenraven, telling the story of her simple
yet stirring life to an absorbed listener ? Yes, without a shadow of conceit he might certainly conclude
that she would prefer an intelligent companion like
himself to that cross-grained boy ; but he had very little to nourish conceit upon in the recollection of the
delightful *tête-à-tête* he had enjoyed. Never before
had he met a woman so free from the indescribable
consciousness by which the gentler sex acknowledge
the presence of the stranger. She must have been
much in the society of men, and of men, too, who
were not lovers. Yet stop ! How much of her composure and frankness was due to the fact of her being
already wooed and promised to one of those con-
founded *carbonari* fellows ? The very idea made
Wilton double-thong his leader—for tandem stages
had been thought necessary—to the infinite surprise
of his servant. However, he reached his destination
at last, and as he threw off his plaid in the hall Mrs.
McKollop's broad and beaming face appeared at
a side-door.

" Aweel, sir, din ye win ower a' right to Brosedale

wi' the young leddy? I've been aye watching the weather; for I don't think she is just that strong. Eh, sir! but she is a bonnie bird—sae saft and kind! When she was going, after I had red up her things for her, she says, 'If you are as good a cook as you are a ladies' maid, I am sure Major Moncrief must be pleased with his dinners,' says she; an' wi' that she takes this neckerchief from her pretty white throat, and says she, so gentle and so grand, 'Wear this for me, Mrs. McKollop,' putting it round my neck her ainsel'. 'Think, whenever ye put it on,' says she, that I shall always remember your motherly care.' The bonnie bird! I'm thinking she has nae mither, or they wouldn't let her be worrit wi' that ill-faured, ill-tempered bairn at Brosedale."

"I left Miss Rivers quite safe, I assure you, and, as far as I could observe, quite well, at the door." said Wilton, who had listened with much attention to this long speech, looking all the time at the pretty violet necktie held up in triumph by Mrs. McKollop, and conscious of a boyish but strong inclination to purchase it, even at a high premium, from the worthy house-keeper. "I am sure you did your best for our charming visitor."

"That I did; an' I tauld her that it was a pleasure to cook for the colonel; for though she spoke of the major, it was aye *you* she thocht on."

"Oh, nonsense!" returned Wilton, good-humoredly, and he left the eloquent Mrs. McKollop, to join
the moody Moncrief, with whom he exchanged but
few remarks, till dinner thawed them. The evening
passed much as usual, but neither mentioned their
guest—a fact by no means indicating that she was
forgotten by either.

CHAPTER VI

WILTON was true to his intention, and rode over the next day to make the promised inquiry, when he had the pleasure of spending half an hour with Donald, but Ella Rivers never appeared. The boy was in one of his better moods, although that was a poor consolation.

"I thought Ella was never coming back yesterday," he said, in his plaintive, querulous voice. "I could not make out whether she had been lost in the snow, or whether your cousin, that Mr. St. George Wilton, had run away with her. Oh! I had such a miserable day!—Miss Walker fussing in and out, and no one able to do anything for me! Where did you pick up Ella?"

"On that piece of common half-way to Monkscleugh; and it is very fortunate I did so, or perhaps you might have been obliged to do without her for some time longer. I fear she would have lost her way altogether."

"Oh, she knows the country, and has plenty of pluck."

"Still, she might have been wandering about for hours, and I fancy she is not over strong."

"She is well enough! Every one is well enough but me!"

"I suppose," said Wilton, to change the subject, "the rest of your party return to-morrow?"

"I am afraid they do! I wish they would stay away! They have taken me up disgustingly since *you* came to see me. I was much happier alone with Ella! I don't mind *your* coming—you are not a humbug; but I hate Helen, she is so insolent; and that cousin of yours is detestable. He is so conceited—so ready to make allowance for everyone. And then he always speaks Italian to Ella, and worries her; I know he does, though she will not tell me what he says."

The boy's words struck an extraordinary pang to Wilton's heart. Had Ella met this diplomatic sprig in Italy? Had he the enormous advantage of having known her and her father in their old free wandering days? If so, why had she not mentioned him? The irrepressible answer to this sprang up with the query —whatever her antecedents, Ella spoke out of the depths of a true soul.

"Well," exclaimed Wilton, while these thoughts revolved themselves, "if you do not like him, do not let him come in here. But I thought he was a universal genius, and an utterly fascinating fellow!"

"The women think so," returned young Fergusson, with an air of superior wisdom, "but I think him a nuisance. Will you ring the bell, Colonel Wilton?"

"What has become of Miss Rivers?" to the servant, who quickly appeared. "Tell her to come here."

Though disposed to quarrel with the terms of the message, Wilton awaited the result with some anxiety. The reply was, "Miss Walker's compliments; Miss Rivers was hearing Miss Isabel read Italian, and she could not come just yet."

"It is infamous!" exclaimed Donald, working himself into a fury. "They all take her from me—they don't care what becomes of me! Give me my crutches, James. I will go to the school-room myself; so I shall say good-by to you, Colonel."

He dragged himself out of the room with surprising rapidity, and Wilton felt he must not stay.

The rest of the day was rendered restless and uncomfortable by Donald's words. But Wilton, though of a passionate and eager nature, had also a strong will, and was too reasonable not to determine resolutely to banish the tyrannic idea which had taken such possession of his heart or imagination. He

9

noticed, with mingled resentment and amusement, the sudden silence and reserve of his friend Moncrief on the subject of Brosedale and its inhabitants. What an absurd, strait-laced old Puritan he was growing! Wilton felt it would be a relief when he departed to pay his promised visit in the South. So, as the weather, after the memorable snow-storm, moderated, and proved favorable for sport, hunting and shooting were resumed with redoubled vigor, and the Major's solemn looks gradually cleared up.

"I shall be rather in the blues here when you are gone," said Wilton, as they sat together the evening before the Major was to leave. "You have not been the liveliest companion in the world of late, still I shall miss you, old boy."

The Major gave an inarticulate grunt, without removing his cigar from his lips.

"So," continued Wilton, "as Lord D—— asks me over to dine and stay a few days while General Loftus and another Crimean man are there, I shall go; and perhaps I may look up the 15th afterwards; they are quartered at C——."

"Do!" said the Major, emphatically, and with unusual animation. "There's nothing more mischievous than moping along and getting into the blue devils!—nothing more likely to drive a man to suicide or matrimony, or some infernal entanglement

even worse ! ' Go over to D—— Castle by all means
—go and have a jolly week or two with the 15th;
and, if you will take my advice, do not return here."

"My dear Moncrief," interrupted Wilton coolly,
for he was a little nettled at the rapid disposal of his
time, "why should I not return here ? What mischief
do you fear for me ? Don't turn enigmatical at this
time of day."

"What mischief do I fear ? The worst of all—a
fair piece of mischief! Not so pretty, perhaps, but
' devilish atthractive,' as poor O'Connor used to say."

Wilton was silent a moment, to keep his temper
quiet. He felt unspeakably annoyed. Anything less
direct he could have laughed off or put aside, but to
touch upon such a subject in earnest galled him to
the quick. To be suspected of any serious feeling
toward Ella necessitated either appearing an idiot
in the eyes of a man like Moncrief--an idiot capable
of throwing away his future for the sake of a freak of
passion—or as entertaining designs more suited to
worldly wisdom, yet which it maddened him to think
any man dared to associate with a creature that somehow or other had managed to establish herself upon
a pedestal, such as no other woman had ever occupied, in his imagination.

"I think," said he at last—and Moncrief was
struck by the stern resentment in his tone—" I think

that too much shooting has made you mad! What, in the name of Heaven, are you talking of? Do you think I am the same unlicked cub you took in hand twelve or fourteen years ago? If you and I are to be friends, let me find my own road through the jungle of life."

"All right," said the Major, philosophically. "Go your own way. I wash my hands of you."

"It is your best plan," returned Wilton, dryly; and the evening passed rather heavily.

The next morning Major Moncrief took leave of his friend. They parted with perfect cordiality, and Wilton drove him over to Monkscleugh.

It is by no means clear that the Major's well-meant warning did the least good. The vexation it caused helped to keep the subject working in Wilton's mind. Certain it was, that after returning from Monkscleugh and writing two or three letters, he took advantage of a fine wintry afternoon to stroll leisurely to the brae before mentioned, and beyond it, to the piece of border ground between the Brosedale plantations and the road, where he had held his horse for Ella Rivers to sketch; but all was silent and deserted, so he returned to dress and drive over to D—— Castle.

It was a pleasant party, and Wilton was a most agreeable addition. He felt at home and at ease with the Earl's kindly, well-bred daughters; and perhaps they would have been a little surprised, could they have read his thoughts, to find that he classed them as unaffected gentlewomen almost equal to the humble companion of Sir Peter Fergusson's crippled boy.

Parties like this, of which Ralph Wilton formed one, are so much alike that it is unnecessary to describe the routine. The third day of his visit the Brosedale family came to dinner, and with them St. George Wilton. Notwithstanding Sir Peter's wealth and Lady Fergusson's fashion, invitations to D—— Castle were few and far between; nor did Ralph Wilton's position as a visitor in the house—a favored, honored guest—seem of small importance in Helen Saville's eyes.

Wilton took her down to dinner, with a sort of friendly glow pervading his manner, well calculated to deceive the object of his attentions. He was dimly aware that, after all his reasoning, all his struggles for self-control, his dominant idea was that if Miss Saville was not the rose, she lived with her.

" I have never seen you since the coming of age at Brantwood ; you have been out when I called, and in when I rode about in search of you—in short, you have scarce cast me a crumb of notice since my polyglot cousin has taken up the running and left me nowhere," said Wilton, under the general buzz of talk, while the chief butler whispered a confidential query as to whether he would have hock or champagne.

"If you will not come in search of the crumbs, you cannot expect to get them," said Miss Saville, looking boldly into his eyes with a smile. "Mamma asked you to dinner the day after our return, but in vain."

"Ah! that day I knew we were to hunt with the ——, and I feared I should not be able to reach Brosedale in time for dinner. Now, tell me, how is every one? Your sister—I mean the school-room one —I see my opposite neighbor is flourishing. How is young Fergusson?"

"Isabel has a cold; but Donald has been wonderfully well. I think we cheer him up! Benevolence seems to run in your family, Colonel Wilton. You set the example, and Mr. St. George Wilton followed it up. Now, we are so anxious to amuse Donald that we congregate on wet, stormy mornings or afternoons in his room, and try to draw—are fearfully snubbed by the young heir! and silently endured by his little companion, who is such a strange girl! By the way, your cousin seems to have known some of her clique abroad. He says they were a dreadful set of communists and freethinkers."

"Indeed," he returned carelessly, as he raised his glass to his lips and made a mental note of the information. "And, pray, how much longer do you intend to foster my delightful relative in the genial warmth of Brosedale?"

"As long as he likes to stay; but he talks of leaving next week."

"Ah! he finds it difficult to tear himself away?"

"That I know nothing about. How long do you remain here?"

"Till the day after to-morrow."

"Then you had better dine with us on the twentieth. I know mamma intends to ask you. The Brantwood party are to be with us, and some people we met at Scarborough last autumn."

"Of course I shall be most happy."

Now there was nothing Wilton hated more than dining at Brosedale; the artificial tone of the house was detestable, and he was always tantalized by knowing that although under the same roof with Ella, he had not the least chance of seeing her; nevertheless, he was impelled to go by a vague, unreasonable hope that some chance might bring about a meeting; and now as he had absolutely written to his old friends of the 15th to say he would be with them the ensuing week, he felt ravenously eager to encounter the very danger from which he had determined to fly. But Helen Saville's hint had filled him with curiosity and uneasiness. It was as he feared. St. George Wilton and Ella Rivers had doubtless many experi-

ences in common which both might prefer talking
about in a tongue unfamiliar to the rest of the audience, for he d'd not, of course, attach any value to
Donald's remark that Ella did not like the clever
attaché. Why should she not like him? He looked
across the table and studied his kinsman's face very
carefully while Ellen Saville told him of a run she
had enjoyed with the ——shire hounds while staying
at Brantwood.

St. George Wilton was occupied in the agreeable
task of entertaining Lady Mary Mowbray, so his
cousin could observe him with impunity. He was a
slight, delicate-looking man, with high, aristocratic
features, pale, with fair hair and light eyes, thin-
lipped, and nominally near-sighted, which entitled
him to use a glass. He wore the neatest possible
moustaches and imperial, and when he smiled, which
was not often (though his face was always set in an
amiable key), he showed a row of very regular white
teeth, but rather too pointed withal, especially the
molars, which were slightly longer than the rest,
and gave a somewhat wolfish, fang-like expression to
that otherwise bland performance. His voice was
carefully modulated, his accent refined, and his ease
of manner the perfection of art. St. George Wilton,
an ambitious poor gentleman, determined to push
his way upwards and onwards, had no doubt sufficient

experience to sharpen and harden his faculties. The
struggle of such a career ought to be, and is invig-
orating; but there are ingredients which turn this
tonic to poison—the greed for wealth and rank, the
hunger for self-indulgence and distinction, the care-
fully-hidden envy that attributes the success of others
to mere good-luck, and curses blind fortune while
congratulating the competitor who has shot ahead
—the gradually increasing tendency to regard all
fellow-creatures as stepping stones or obstacles—the
ever-growing, devouring self which, after rejecting
every joy that gladdens by reciprocity, slowly starves
to death in the Sahara of its own creation.

Although the cousins had seldom met before, they
had heard of each other, forming their respective esti-
mates from their special standpoints—St. George
heartily despising Ralph, as a mere stupid, honest,
pig-headed soldier, whose luck in coming somewhat
to the front was a disgrace even to the whims of that
feminine deity, Fortune. How such rapid promotion
could be brought about without finesse, without tact,
without anything more extraordinary than simple duty
doing, was beyond the peculiar construction of St.
George's mind to conceive. While Ralph scarcely
bestowed any consideration whatever on his kinsman
—he had heard of him as a clever, rising man, and
also as a "keen hand;" but now he had acquired a

sudden importance; and Ralph, as he gazed at the bland countenance opposite, and traced the hard lines under its set expression, laughed inwardly at the notion of extracting any information which St. George was disinclined to give.

Nevertheless, when they joined the ladies, Wilton approached his cousin, and opened the conversation by inquiring for a mutual acquaintance, one of St. George's brother *attachés*; this naturally led to other topics, and their talk flowed easily enough. "I am told you were received by our eccentric relative, Lord St. George," said his namesake, at last; "rather an unusual event for him to see any one, I believe?"

"Yes; he sent for me, or I should never have thought of presenting myself. He looks very old and worn—and not particularly amiable."

"Well, he has had enough to sour him. How did he receive you?"

"With tolerable civility."

"He would not let me in! I wonder what he will do with all his property. If he dies intestate, I suppose you will inherit everything?"

"I suppose so; but I strongly suspect he will not leave me a *sou.* I am not pliant enough; and that unfortunate daughter of his may have left children to inherit, after all. I fancy I heard she was dead."

"So have I," said St. George. "Who did she marry?"

"I believe a Spaniard—an adventurer, with fine eyes and a splendid voice; I forget the name. Old Colonel du Cane, who was about town in those days, remembers the affair and the scandal, but the whole thing is forgotten now. I wonder old St. George did not marry and cut out every one."

"Unless he makes a very distinct will, you will have to spend a large slice of your fortune in defeating the pretenders who are sure to spring up."

"Or you will," returned Wilton, laughing; "for he is as likely to leave it to one as the other, or to some charity."

"To some charity? That is surely the last of improbabilities."

"It is impossible to say," returned Wilton; and there was a short pause, during which he revolved rapidly in his own mind how he could best approach the topic uppermost in his mind. "How long do you stay at Brosedale?" he resumed abruptly, as St. George looked round, as if about to move away.

"Perhaps a week longer. I have already paid a visitation, but the house is comfortable, the girls agreeable, and the *padrone* unobtrusive."

"If you had not been in such luxurious quarters, and enjoying such excellent sport, I should have asked you to try a day or two on the moor I have at Glenraven."

"Thank you; I should have been most happy, but am engaged to Lord Parchmount after the twenty-fifth."

"Did you ever meet any of Lady Fergusson's people, the Savilles she is so fond of talking about; I fancy there was a brother of hers in the —th Hussars?"

"A brother of her former husband's, you mean. I don't believe Lady Fergusson ever had a brother or a father, or any blood tie of any kind, but sprang up full-blown, lovely, ambitious, aristocratic, at the touch of some magic wand; or, to come to a commonplace simile, in a single night's growth, like a toad-stool. She has been eminently successful too. What a catch Sir Peter was! Now, if that wretched boy were to die—for which consummation, no doubt, her ladyship devoutly prays—and Helen Saville would play her cards with the commonest discretion, she might secure the fortune for herself and her sisters; but she is a very uncertain person, a woman on whom no one could count." And St. George shook his head, as though he had given the subject mature consideration.

"I suppose you have seen the son and heir?" asked Wilton.

"Frequently. He dislikes me, and I am amused at the elaborate display he makes of it. I also like to air my Italian with his interesting little companion."

"You knew her in Italy, I think Miss Saville said," remarked Wilton.

"Knew her? Never. I fancy, from what she says, I have met some of the people her father associated with—a very disreputable set."

"Sharpers and blacklegs, I suppose," said Wilton carelessly.

"No; politically disreputable; dreamers of utopian dreams, troublesome items to governments; amiable men, who will make martyrs of themselves. You have no idea in England what a nuisance these fellows are; of course there are plenty of desperate fanatics mixed up with them. I do not remember the name of Rivers among those I have met, but I imagine that picturesque girl at Brosedale was among the better class. She really looks like a gentlewoman; with her knowledge of language and air of refinement she would make a charming travelling companion."

As the accomplished *attaché* uttered this with a soft arch smile, as though it were an infantine jest, he little thought what a large amount of self-control he called into action in his cousin's mind. To have seized him by the collar, and shaken him till he retracted the insulting words, would have been a great relief; to have rebuked him sternly for speaking lightly of a girl of whom he knew no evil, would have been some satisfaction; but modern manners forbade the first, and a due sense of the ridiculous the second. Control himself as Wilton might, he could not call up the answering smile which St. George expected, but instead stared at him with a fixed haughty stare, which, although rather unaccountable to its object, seemed sufficiently disagreeable to make him turn away and seek more congenial companionship.

Wilton, too, talked and laughed, and played his part with a proper degree of animation; but a bruised, galled sensation clung to him all the evening. There is a large class of men for whom such a remark as St. George Wilton's would have been fatally destructive to the charm and romance enfolding an object of admiration. To find what is precious to them, common and unholy in the eyes of another, would destroy the preciousness and desecrate the holiness! But there is another, a smaller, though nobler and stronger class, whom the voice of the scoffer, scoff he never so subtly, cannot incite to doubt or disloyalty—to whom love is still lovely, and beauty still beautiful; although others apply different terms to what they have recognized as either one or the other. These are the men who see with their own eyes, and· Wilton was one of them. It was with the sort of indignation a crusader might have felt to see an infidel handling a holy relic, that he thought of his cousin's careless words. Nay, more, reflecting that St. George was but one of many who would have thus felt and spoken of a girl to whom he dared not address a word of love lest it might check or destroy the sweet, frank friendliness with which she treated him, he asked himself again, what was to bé the end thereof? Then he for the first time acknowledged to himself what he had often indistinctly felt before, that to tell her he loved her, to ask her to be his wife, to read astonishment, perhaps dawning tenderness, in her wonderful eyes, to hold her to his heart, to own her before the world, to shelter her from difficulty so far as one mortal can another, would be heaven to him!

She had struck some deeper, truer chord in his nature than had ever been touched before ; and his whole being answered ; all that seemed impossible and insurmountable gradually faded into insignificance compared to his mighty need for that quiet, pale, dark-eyed little girl!

The day after Wilton's return from D——Castle, feeling exceedingly restless and unaccountably expectant, he sallied forth with his gun on his shoulder, more as any excuse than with any active sporting intentions. As he passed the gate into the road, a large half-bred mastiff, belonging to Sir Peter Fergusson, rushed up, and Wilton, knowing he was an ill-tempered brute, called his own dogs to heel, but the mastiff did not notice them; he kept snuffing about as though he had lost his master, and then set off in a long, swinging gallop toward Brosedale.

Wilton, deep in thought, went on to the brae he so often visited in the commencement of his stay at Glenraven. He had not long quitted the high road, when he perceived a well-known figure, as usual clothed in gray, walking rather slowly before him, and looking wonderfully in accordance with the soft, neutral tints of sky and stones and hill-side—it was one of those still, mild winter days that have in them something of the tenderness and resignation of old age ; and which, in our variable climate, sometimes come with a startling change of atmosphere immediately after severe cold. As he hastened to overtake her, Wilton fancied her step was less firm and elastic than usual ; that her head drooped slightly as if depressed ; yet there was a little more color than was ordinary in her cheek, and certainly an expression of pleasure in her eyes that made his heart beat when she turned at his salutation. She wore a small turban hat of black velvet, with a rosette in front, which looked Spanish, and most becoming to her dark eyes and pale, refined face.

"At last, Miss Rivers ! I thought you must have abjured this brae since Moncrief and myself became temporary proprietors. I began to fear I should never meet you out of doors again."

"I have not been out for a long time alone," she replied ; "but to-day some great man from London, a doctor, was to see poor Donald, and I was free for awhile, so I rambled away far up that hill-side. It was delightful—so still, so grave, so soft."

"You have been up the hill," cried Wilton, infinitely annoyed to think he had been lounging and writing in the house when he might have had a long walk with his companion. "I wish I had been with you. I imagine it must double one's enjoyment of scenery to look at it with a thorough artist like yourself."

Miss Rivers did not reply at once, but, after a moment's pause, asked, "Are you going out now to shoot ? "

"Well, yes—at least it is my first appearance to-day."

"Would it be very inconvenient to you to walk back to Brosedale, or part of the way, with me ?" She spoke with a slight, graceful hesitation.

"Inconvenient! No, certainly not," returned Wilton, trying to keep his eyes and voice from expressing too plainly the joy her request gave him. "It is a charity to employ me. You know I have lost my chum, Major Moncrief, and I feel somewhat adrift. But I thought young Fergusson was better. Miss Saville said so."

Miss Rivers shook her head. "They know nothing about it. He will never be better; but it is not because he is worse that this great doctor comes. He pays periodical visits. Donald always suffers; and I think he frets because his step-sisters and that cousin of yours come and sketch and talk in our room so often; it does him no good."

"Am I wrong in interpreting your emphasis on '*that* cousin of yours' as an unfavorable expression?"

"Do you like him?" she asked, looking straight into his eyes.

"No," replied Wilton, uncompromisingly; while he gave back her gaze with interest.

"It is curious," she said, musingly, "for he never offends; he is accomplished; his voice is pleasant. Why do you not like him?"

"I cannot tell. Why don't you?"

"Ah! it is different. I—I am foolish, perhaps, to be so influenced by unreasoning instinct; but I fancy—I feel—he is not honest—not true. Are you really kinsmen?—of the same race, the same blood?"

"Yes, I believe so! And may I infer from your question that you believe I am tolerably honest—beyond deserving to be intrusted with the forks and spoons, I mean?"

"I do—I do, indeed." She spoke quite earnestly, and the words made Wilton's heart beat. Before, however, he had time to reply, a gentleman came round an angle of broken bank, crowned by a group of mountain ash, which in summer formed a very picturesque point, and to Wilton's great surprise he found himself face to face with St. George. Involuntarily he looked at Ella Rivers, but she seemed not in the least astonished ; rather cold and collected. Suddenly it flashed into his mind that she had asked his escort to avoid a *t te-à-t'te* with the agreeable *attaché*, with a crowd of associated inferences not calculated to increase his cousinly regard. St. George raised his hat with a gentle smile.

"I did not expect to have the pleasure of meeting you, Colonel, though I had intended paying you a visit. Miss Rivers, one has seldom a chance of finding you so far afield. I presume it is a favorable indication of the young laird's health that you can be spared to enjoy a ramble with Colonel Wilton."

There was just the suspicion of a sneer about his lips as he spoke, which completed the measure of Wilton's indignation. But Miss Rivers replied with the most unmoved composure that Donald was as usual, and then walked on in silence. After a few remarks, very shortly answered by Wilton, the bland *attaché* accepted his defeat.

"Did you see a large brown dog along here? I had the brute with me this morning, and he has strayed.

I do not like to return without him, for he is rather a favorite with Sir Peter."

"Yes, I saw him just now further up the road, close to my gate," returned Wilton quickly, without adding what direction the animal had taken.

"Thank you. Then I will prosecute my search instead of spoiling your *tête-à-tête*"—with which parting shot St. George left them.

For some paces Wilton and his companion walked on in silence. He stole a glance at her face; it was composed and thoughtful. "I suppose you were not surprised by that apparition? Perhaps it was a choice of the smaller evil that induced you to adopt a *tête-à-tête* with me, instead of with him?" He looked earnestly for her reply.

"It was," she said, without raising her eyes to his. "He passed me just now in the dog-cart with another gentleman, and I thought it possible he might return; so, as you have always been kind and friendly, I thought I might ask you to come with me."

Another pause ensued, for Wilton's heated imagination conjured up an array of serious annoyances deserving the severest castigation, and he scarcely dared trust himself to speak, so fearful was he of checking her confidence, or seeming to guess too much of the truth. At last he exclaimed, with a sort of suppressed vehemence that startled Miss Rivers

into looking at him quickly, " By heaven, it is too bad
that you should be bored, in your rare moments of
freedom, with the idle chatter of that fellow."

" It is a bore, but that is all. It amuses him to
speak Italian with me "—an expression of superb dis-
dain gleamed over her face for an instant, and left it
quiet and grave. " Though wonderfully civil, even
complimentary, he conveys, more than any one I ever
met, the hatefulness of class distinctions."

" I feel deeply thankful for the doubt you expressed
just now that he belonged to the same race as myself."

" You are quite different ; but I dare say you have
plenty of the prejudices peculiar to your caste."

" I wish you would undertake my conversion. It
might not be so difficult. Your denunciation of
soldiers has rung in my ears—no—rather haunted my
imagination ever since you showed me your sketch-
book in that desolate waiting-room."

" I remember," said she, gravely. " No, I shall
never convert you ; even if I wrote a political thesis
for your benefit." After a short pause, she resumed
abruptly, " Do you know, I fear poor Donald has not
much of life before him ? "

" Indeed ! What induces you to think so ? "

" He is so weak, and feverish, and sleepless. He
often rings for me to read to him in the dead of the
night. And then, with all his ill temper and selfish-

ness, he has at times such gleams of noble thought, such flashes of intellectual light, that I cannot help feeling it is the flicker of the dying lamp. I shall be profoundly grieved when his sad, blighted life is over. No one knows him as I do ; and no one cares for me as he does. I have ventured to speak to Lady Fergusson, but she cannot or will not see, and forbids my addressing Sir Peter on the subject."

"And if this unfortunate boy dies, what is to become of you?" asked Wilton, too deeply interested to choose his words, yet a little apprehensive lest he might offend.

"I do not know; I have never thought," she replied, quite naturally. "I suppose I should go back to Mrs. Kershaw. She is fond of me in her way, especially since I nursed her through that fever."

"And then," persisted Wilton, looking earnestly at her half-averted face with an expression which, had she turned and caught it, would probably have destroyed the pleasant, friendly tone of their intercourse.

"I do not know; but I do not dread work. To do honest service is no degradation to me. I have always heard of work as the true religion of humanity. No. I have very little fear of the future, because, perhaps, I have so little hope."

"You are a strange girl," exclaimed Wilton, with a certain degree of familiarity, which yet was perfectly respectful. "I fancy few men have so much pluck I dare say Lady Fergusson would not like to lose so charming a companion for her daughters."

"Lady Fergusson does not think me at all charming; and Miss Saville does not like me, nor I her. But whether they like it or not, I shall not remain if Donald dies."

"Mrs. Kershaw is the person in whose house your father died?" said Wilton softly, and in the same confidential tone their conversation had taken.

Miss Rivers bent her head.

"Where does she live?"

"At Kensington."

"Whereabouts? I know Kensington pretty well."

"Oh! in H—— Street. There is a little garden in front, so it is called Gothic Villa, though there is very little that is Gothic about it." Here Miss Rivers stopped.

"Yes!" exclaimed Wilton; "I see we are within the Brosedale boundaries; but you must not dismiss your escort yet; that diplomatic relative of mine may be on our heels."

"Do not imagine I fear to encounter him," said she, with an arch smile. "I ought, perhaps, to apologize to you for taking you out of your way for so slight a cause; but even if a fly alights on one's brow or hand, the impulse is to brush it away."

"Do not dismiss me so soon, however. I am going away the day after to-morrow, and may not see you again before I leave."

"You are going! I am sorry." She spoke with a simple sincerity that at once charmed, and yet mortified him.

"You have always seemed more like an old friend than a stranger," she continued; "and I shall miss you."

"If I could be of the smallest use—the slightest comfort to you," said Wilton—his tones deepening unconsciously while he drew nearer to her, feeling still fearful of awakening any consciousness of the passionate feeling with which he regarded her—"I would willingly renounce my visit to A——; but I am only going there for a few days, and hope to return in time for some entertainment which is to take place in honor of Sir Peter's birthday."

"Oh, yes; it was the same last year. A ball for the near neighbors and tenants and dwellers in the house. I had no heart to see the last, but I have promised Isabel to be present at this."

"Indeed! then, pray, make another promise—to dance with me."

"Yes; I will dance with you, if you remember about it, and come to claim me."

"If!" repeated Wilton with eloquent emphasis;

"If I am in life you will see me there, even though I risk another railway smash to keep the tryst."

There was a fervor and depth in his voice beyond what the mere words required that struck his companion. She turned to him with a startled, wondering expression in her eyes, which met his fully for a moment, and then sank slowly, while a faint flitting blush came and went on her cheek, the sweet curved lips quivered, and an unmistakable look of pain and gravity stole over her face. Wilton was ready to curse his own want of self-control for thus disturbing her, and yet this touch of emotion and consciousness completed the potent spell she had laid upon him. He burned to complete with his lips the confession his eyes had begun, but he must not, dare not then; so, with an immense effort over himself, he managed to say somewhat at random, "I suppose they have a good band—good enough to dance to?"

"Yes, I believe so;" and then again she stood still. "You have come quite far enough. I must say good-by. I do not wish to take you any further." She again raised her eyes to his with a sort of effort, but gravely and resolutely.

"I obey," replied Wilton as gravely, all anxiety to win her back to her former easy, confidential tone; he raised his hat and looked in vain for a movement

on her side to hold out her hand. "Then I may
count on you for the first waltz at the birthday fête.
I shall come for it, rest assured ; so remember if you
let St. George or any one else persuade you to break
your promises, the results may be—fatal." He
endeavored to assume a light tone, but could not
judge of its effect, for Miss Rivers merely said in a
low voice, "Good-by. I shall not forget."

Wilton sought for another glance in vain. She
bent her head as he stood aside to let her pass, and
vanished quickly among the trees.

The walk back was accomplished almost unconsciously, so deeply was Wilton absorbed in thought.
Involuntarily he had torn away the veil which had
hitherto hidden the real character of their intercourse from that proud, frank, simple girl, and how
would she take it ? With a woman of her calibre anything like indirectness, of parleying with generous
impulses, would consign him to the limbo of her contempt ; and the grand scorn of her face when she
spoke of St. George Wilton amusing himself with her,
flashed back upon him. Of that he could not bear to
think, nor of giving her up and seeking safety in
flight, nor of tormenting himself by hanging about her
vaguely. There was but one way out of it all— wild,
imprudent; insane as it must appear, even to decent
worldlings like Moncrief—and that was to go in gal-

7*

lantly and dauntlessly for marriage at all risks. Wilton's pulses throbbed at the idea; once certain of himself and his motives, he felt that he could break down any barrier of reserve Ella Rivers might erect against him, and, at least, ascertain what were his chances, or if he had any.

In this mood the next day's dinner at Brosedale was a great trial, though a slight increase of friendliness toward St. George, who had evidently held his tongue about their rencontre. All passed over serenely, and promising faithfully to return in time for the ball, he bid the Brosedale party "good-night." Not sorry to try his own impressions by the test of change, both of scene and company, he started for A—— the next morning.

CHAPTER VII.

THE annual entertainment at Brosedale was on an unusual scale this year. The house was full, and full of eligible people. Mr. St. George Wilton, it is true, had departed without laying himself and his diplomatic honors at Miss Saville's feet; but that accomplished young lady was upheld by the consciousness that his soldier-cousin would be there to fill his place, and would be no mean substitute.

This celebration of Sir Peter Fergusson's birthday was instituted by his admiring wife, who found it useful as a sort of rallying point at a difficult season, and helped the family radiance to obliterate the whilom revered Grits of Brosedale; and Sir Peter, to whom money was no object, allowed himself to be flattered and fooled into this piece of popularity-hunting as "advisable" and the "right thing.".

Wilton dressed and drove over to Brosedale, in a mingled state of resolution and anxiety. Although he seemed as pleasant a companion, as good a shot, as bold a rider as ever to his Hussar hosts, he found plenty of time to think, to examine, and to torment

himself. He had not reached his thirty-fifth year without a sprinkling of love affairs, some of them, especially of early date, fiery enough; but no previous fancy
or passion had taken such deep hold upon him as the
present one. Like many of the better sort of men,
he looked on women as pretty, charming toys; to
be kindly and honorably treated, cared for and pro-
tected, but chiefly created for man's pleasure, to give
a certain grace to his existence when good, and to
spoil it when wicked. A woman with convictions,
with an individual inner life; a woman he could talk
to, as to a friend, apart from her personal attraction;
a woman who spoke to him as if love-making was not
thought of between them; a woman to whom he dared
not make love lest he should lose those delicious
glimpses of heart and mind, so fresh, so utterly unconscious of their own charm—this was something quite
beyond his experience. Then, to a true gentleman,
her strangely forlorn, isolated position hedged her
round with a strong though invisible fence; and the
great difficulty of meeting her alone, of finding opportunities to win her, and rouse her from her pleasant
but provoking ease and friendliness—all conspired
to fan the steadily increasing fire. Occupy himself as
he might, the sound of her voice was ever in his ear;
her soft, earnest, fearless eyes forever in his sight.
What a companion she would be, with her bright

intelligence, her quick sympathy, her artistic taste! and through all this attraction of fancy and intelligence ran the electric current of strong passion, the intense longing to read love in her eyes, to feel the clasp of her slender arms, to hold her to his heart, and press his lips to hers! He had known many fairer women, but none before had stirred his deeper, better nature like this friendless, obscure girl, on whom he involuntarily looked with more of reverence than the haughtiest peeress had called forth; and come what might, he would not lose her for lack of boldness to face the possible ills of an unequal match.

Wilton did not deceive himself as to the seeming insanity of such a marriage. He knew what Moncrief would say; what the world in which he lived would say—for that he cared little; but he looked ahead. He knew his means were limited for a man in his position; then there were good appointments in India and elsewhere for military men with administrative capacities and tolerable interest; and with Ella Rivers and plenty of work, home and happiness would exist anywhere, everywhere! Lord St. George! Ay; there lay a difficulty. However, he was certainly a perfectly free agent; but it went sorely against him to resign the prospect of wealth to support the rank which must come to him. Insensibly he had appropriated it in his mind since his interview with the old peer,

and now he wished more than ever to secure it for
Ella's sake. Whatever might be the obscurity of her
origin, she would give new dignity to a coronet, if she
would accept him. It was this "if" that lay at the
root of the anxiety with which Wilton drove to Brosedale, and struggled to be lively and agreeable while
the guests assembled, for he was unusually early.
Who could foresee whether that wonderful unconsciousness which characterized Miss Rivers's manner
might not be the result of a preoccupied heart? At
the idea of a rival—a successful rival—Wilton felt
murderous, while smiling and complimenting Miss
Saville as they stood together in the music-room, where
the first arrivals were received.

"I thought St. George had left some time ago,"
he said, observing that gentleman approach.

"He returned for the ball," replied Miss Saville,
who was looking very handsome in a superb toilet.
"He dances divinely. We could not have got on
without him."

"Dancing is a diplomatic accomplishment," said
Wilton gravely. "I am told there used to be a com-
petition ballet once a year at Whitehall, for which leave
was granted at remote missions; but the advantages
possessed by the Paris and Vienna *attachés* over those
in Vancouver's Land and the Cannibal Islands were

so unfair that it has been discontinued; besides, old H—— is opposed to the graces."

This speech permitted St. George to come up, and he immediately engaged the beautiful Helen for the first waltz.

"I think we may as well begin, Helen," said Lady Fergusson; "we can make up two or three quadrilles. "Come, Lord Ogilvie"—this to a fledgling lord, who had been caught for the occasion—"take Miss Saville to the ball-room."

"Where is your youngest daughter, Lady Fergusson?" asked Colonel Wilton. "I suppose on such an occasion she is permitted to share the pomps and vanities. Eh?"

"Oh, Isabel! She has already gone into the ball-room with Miss Walker; but I cannot permit you to throw yourself away on a school girl. Let me introduce you to—"

"My dear Lady Fergusson, you must permit me the liberty of choice. Isabel or nothing," he interrupted.

"Very well," said Lady Fergusson, with a slight, but pleased smile.

Colonel Wilton offered his arm, and they proceeded to the ball-room. It was the largest of two large drawing-rooms, only separated by handsome columns. Cleared of furniture and profusely decorated with flowers, it was spacious and attractive enough to satisfy the wildest D——shire imagination, nor was it beneath the approval of the experienced Londoners staying in the house. At one end it opened on a large fragrant conservatory ; here the band was stationed ; at the further end of the second drawing-room was an apartment devoted to refreshments, and again communicating with the conservatory by a glass-covered passage lined with tropical shrubs, lighted by soft, ground-glass lamps, and warmed to a delicious temperature. When Wilton entered the ball-room the first sets of quadrilles were being formed. He soon perceived Isabel standing beside her step-father, and Miss Walker, in festive attire, conversing with a learned-looking old gentleman in spectacles at a little distance. Wilton's heart failed him. Where was Ella Rivers ? Had Donald insisted on keeping her a prisoner lest she might enjoy a pleasure he could not share ?

However, he asked the delighted school-girl to dance with a suitable air of enjoyment, and before the third figure had begun had extracted the following information.

" Donald has been frightfully cross all day ; he always is when we have a ball ; and he has kept Miss Rivers so late ! But I think she is ready now ; she was to wait in the conservatory till Miss Walker

11

went for her, as she could not very well come in
alone."

After which communication Miss Isabel Saville
found her partner slightly absent, and given rather to
spasmodic spurts of conversation than to continuous
agreeability. In truth, the quadrille seemed very
long. He watched Miss Walker carefully; she was
still alone, and—if such a phrase could be applied to
anything so rigid—fluttering amiably from one dow-
ager to another among the smaller gentry invited
once a year.

"Now Colonel Wilton," said Lady Fergusson
when the quadrille was over, "I will introduce you
to a charming partner—an heiress, a belle—"

"Do not think of it," he interrupted. "I have
almost forgotten how to dance; you had better keep
me as a reserve fund for the partnerless and forlorn."

Wilton stepped back to make way for some new
arrivals; still, no sign of Ella. Miss Walker was in
deep conversation with a stout lady in maroon satin
and black lace; she had evidently forgotten her
promise; so, slipping through the rapidly-increas-
ing crowd, Wilton executed a bold and skilful flank
movement.

Passing behind the prettily ornamented stand
occupied by the musicians, just as they struck up a
delicious waltz, he plunged into the dimly-lighted

recesses of the conservatory in search of the missing girl. She was not there, so he dared to penetrate into the passage before mentioned, on which one or two doors opened ; one of them was open, letting in a brilliant light from the room behind, and just upon the threshold stood Ella Rivers, with an expectant look in her eyes. Wilton paused in his approach, so impressed was he by her air of distinction. The delicate white of her neck and arms showed through her dress of black gauze ; her dark brown, glossy hair braided back into wide plaited loops behind her small shell-like ear, and brought round the head in a sort of crown, against which lay her only ornament, a white camellia with its dark green leaves. As she stood thus, still and composed, waiting patiently, and looking so purely, softly, colorless, and fair, the quiet grace of her figure, the dusk transparency of her drapery, associated her in Wilton's fancy with the tender beauty of moonlight ; but, as the thought passed through his brain, he stepped forward and accosted her.

"I have come to claim the waltz you promised me, Miss Rivers."

She started, and colored slightly. "Yes," she replied, "I am ready, as you have remembered. I am waiting for Miss Walker, who promised to come for me."

"She is engaged with some people in the ball-room, so I ventured to come in her place."

He bowed, and offered his arm as he spoke, with the utmost deference; and Miss Rivers, with one quick, surprised glance, took it in silence.

"You remembered your promise to me?" asked Wilton, as they passed through the conservatory.

"Scarcely," she replied, with a slight smile. "I did not think of it till you spoke."

"And had I been a little later I should have found you waltzing with some more fortunate fellow?"

"Yes, very likely, had any one else asked me. You see," apologetically, "I am very fond of dancing, and I know so few—or rather I know no one—so had you not come, and I had waited for you, I might never have danced at all."

"But you *knew* I would come," exclaimed Wilton, eagerly.

Miss Rivers shook her head, raising her eyes to his with the first approach to anything like coquetry he had ever noticed in her, though playfulness would be the truer description.

"You knew I would come," he repeated.

"Indeed I did not."

These words brought them to the ball-room, and as they stepped out into the light and fragrance of the bright, well-filled, decorated room, Wilton's companion uttered a low exclamation of delight.

"How beautiful! how charming—and the music! Come, let us dance! we are losing time. Oh! how long it is since I danced! How glad I am you came for me!"

Wilton tried to look into her eyes, to catch their expression when she uttered these words, but in vain—they were wandering with animated delight over the gay scene and whirling figures, while her hand, half unconsciously, was stretched up to his shoulder. The next moment they were floating away to the strains of one of Strauss's dreamy waltzes.

"And where did you last dance?" asked Wilton, as they paused for breath.

"Oh! at M——, under the great chestnut trees. There was an Austrian band there; and, although such tyrants, they make excellent music, the Austrians. It was so lovely and fresh that evening."

"And who were your partners—Austrian or Italian?"

"Neither; I only danced with Diego—dear, good Diego. Do not speak of it! I want to forget now. I want to enjoy this one evening—just this one."

There was wonderful pathos in her voice and eyes; but Wilton only said, "Then, if you are rested, we will go on again." He could not trust himself to say more at that moment.

When the dance was ended, Wilton, anxious to avoid drawing any notice upon his partner, led her at once to Miss Walker, and considerably astonished that lady by asking her for the next quadrille. For several succeeding dances he purposely avoided Ella, while he distributed his attentions with judicious impartiality; although he managed to see that she danced more than once, but never with St. George, who seemed to avoid her.

At last, the move to supper was made, and, at the same time, a gay gallop was played, to employ the younger guests and keep them from crowding upon their elders while in the sacred occupation of eating. Seeing the daughters of the house deeply engaged, Wilton indulged himself in another dance with Ella. When they ceased, the room was wellnigh cleared.

"Now, tell me," said Wilton—his heart beating fast, for he was resolved not to part with his companion until he had told her the passionate love which she had inspired—till he had won her to some avowal, or promise, or explanation—"tell me, have you had nothing all this time? No ice, or wine, or—"

"Yes—an ice; it was very good."

"And you would like another? Come, we are more likely to find it in the refreshment-room than at supper, and be less crowded too ; unless your mind is fixed on game pie and champagne?" While he forced himself to speak lightly, he scarce heard his own spoken words, for listening to the burning sentences forming themselves in his brain, and for planning how to find some blessed opportunity of being alone with the fair girl, whose hand, as it rested on his arm, he could not help pressing to his side.

" No, no," she exclaimed, smiling, "I do not care for game pie ; but I should like an ice."

" Then we will make for the refreshment-room." It was nearly empty, but not quite ; one or two couples and a few waiters rendered it anything but a desirable solitude. However, Wilton composed himself as best he could to watch Ella eat her ice, while he solaced himself with a tumbler of champagne. "Who have you been dancing with?" he asked, trying to make her speak and look at him.

" I do not know. One gentleman was introduced to me by Isabel ; the other introduced himself. I liked him the best, although he is a soldier "—a laughing glance at Wilton—"and he says he knows you."

" Oh! young Langley of the 15th, I suppose?"

" He dances very badly—much worse than you do."

" That is a very disheartening speech. I thought I

rather distinguished myself this evening; but I suppose your friend Diego could distance me considerably."

" You mean he danced better?"—pausing, with a spoonful of ice half-way to her lips. " Well, yes; you really dance very well; I enjoyed my dance with you; but Diego! his dancing was superb!"

" Was he not rather old for such capering?"

" Old! Ah, no. Diego never was, never will be, old! Poor fellow! You would like Diego, if you knew him."

" You think so?"—very doubtfully—" however, we were not to talk about him. Let me take away your plate. And have you managed to enjoy your evening?"

" Well, no "—looking up at him with wistful eyes —" that is the truth. It is so terribly strange and lonely, I was thinking of stealing away when you asked me for that galop."

" Let us go and see Donald," exclaimed Wilton, abruptly rising. " His room opens on the other side of the conservatory, does it not?"

" But he is not there; he is gone to bed."

" Had he gone when you came away?"

" No; but he was quite worn out with his own crossness, and is, I hope, fast asleep by this time."

" Well, I am under the impression that he is still up."

"Did any one tell you? How very wrong. He ought to be in bed. I shall go and see."

"Yes; you had better. It is half past twelve! Let me go with you; I may be of some use."

"Come, then," said she, frankly; and Wilton followed her, feeling that he was about to reap the reward of the self-control by which he had won back her confidence, which he feared his unguarded glance had shaken when they had last met.

Ella Rivers walked quickly down the passage leading to the conservatory, now quite deserted, the band having gone to refresh, and crossed to a glass door, through which light still shone. "I do believe he is up. The lamp is still burning." She opened it and stepped in. Wilton followed, dexterously dropping the curtain as he passed through.

"No; he is gone," said Ella, looking around. "I am so glad!"

"So am I," exclaimed Wilton, most sincerely.

"How quiet and comfortable the room looks," continued his companion, drawing off her gloves. "I shall not return to the ball; it is no place for me; so good-night, Colonel Wilton."

"Not yet," he exclaimed, in a low, earnest tone. "Hear me first—I cannot help speaking abruptly—I dare not lose so precious an opportunity." He approached her as he spoke. She was standing by a

large writing-table near the fire-place, where the last
embers were dying out ; she had just laid down her
gloves, and, resting one hand upon the table, looked
up with a wondering, startled expression.   Her total
unconsciousness of what was coming struck Wilton
dumb for a moment ; but he was naturally resolute,
and had the advantage of having thoroughly made up
his mind.   " Although I have done my best to mask
my feelings," he resumed, speaking rapidly, but with
unmistakable emotion, " fearing to frighten you from
the friendly confidence you have hitherto shown me,
I cannot hide or suppress them any longer—I must
tell you I love you !   I must ask if there is a chance
for me with you ?   I know it is audacious to address
you thus when I have had so few opportunities of
making myself known to you ; but the great difficulty
of seeing you, your peculiar position, the terrible
uncertainty—"

   " Oh ! hush, hush !" interrupted Ella, who had
turned very pale, covering her eyes with one hand and
stretching out the other as if to ward off a danger ;
" do not speak like that !   Have I lost my only friend !
I did not dream of this—at least I only once feared
it, I—"

   " Feared," interrupted Wilton in his turn.   " Why,
am I lost ?   Are you pledged to some other man that
you shrink from me ?   Speak, Ella !   If it is so, why

I must not force myself upon you. Speak to me!
look at me!" And, in his intense anxiety to ascertain the truth, he drew her hand from her face and
held it locked in both of his.

"I pledged to any one! no indeed "—raising her
eyes, by a sort of determined effort, gravely. earnestly
to his—"I never thought of such a thing!" she
returned, trying to draw away her hand.

"Then am I utterly unacceptable to you? You
cannot form an idea of the intense love you have
created, or you would not speak so coldly! Ella,
there is no one to care for you as I do—no one to
consult—no one to keep you back from me! If you
do not care for me now, tell me how I can win you!
do not turn away from me! I have much to explain
—much to tell you—and I dare not detain you now
lest we might be interrupted, but come to-morrow
across the brae! I will be there every afternoon by
the cairn until you can manage to come, if you will
only promise. For God's sake do not refuse to hear
me!" He bent over her, longing. yet not daring, to
draw her to him.

"Let my hand go," said Ella, in a low voice. and
trembling very much. Wilton instantly released it.
"Go to meet you! no, I must not—I will not." She
stopped, and, pressing her hand against her heart,
went on hurriedly—"I can hear no more; I will go

away now! Ah! how sorry I am!" She moved
toward a door opening into the house, but Wilton
intercepted her.

"You misunderstand me, though I cannot see
why; but will you at least promise to read what I
write? Promise this, and I will not intrude upon
you any longer."

"I will," she replied faintly. Wilton bowed and
stepped back; the next instant he was alone.

Alone, and most uncomfortable. He had in some
mysterious manner offended her. He could understand her being a little startled, but— here one of those
sudden intuitions which come like a flash of summer
lightning, revealing objects shrouded in the dark of a
sultry night, darted across his misty conjectures—he
had not mentioned the words "wife" or "marriage."
Could she imagine that he was only trifling with her?
or worse? The blood mounted to his cheek as the
thought struck him; and yet, painful as the idea was,
it suggested hope. Her evident grief, her visible
shrinking from the word "love," did not look like
absolute indifference. She did not like to lose him
as a friend, and she feared a possible loss of respect
in his adopting the character of her lover. Then she
had been so deeply impressed by the caste prejudices
of the people around her, to say nothing of the possible
impertinences of Mr. St. George Wilton, that it was

not improbable she had cruelly misinterpreted his
avowal. These reflections gave him the keenest pain,
the most ardent longing to fly to Ella to pour out
assurances of the deepest, the warmest esteem, but
that was impossible for the present; he had nothing
for it but to hook up the curtain again, and return to
the ball-room, planning a letter to Ella, which should
leave no shadow of doubt as to the sincerity and
purity of his affection for her.

But the sound of the music, the sight of the dancers,
the effort to seem as if nothing had happened, was too
much for his self-control, and, excusing himself to his
hostess, he was soon driving home, thankful to be out
in the cold, fresh night air, which seemed to quiet his
pulses and clear his thoughts. Cost him what it
might, he would never give Ella up, unless she positively refused him, and of that he would not think.
The slight and unsatisfactory taste of open love-making
which he had snatched only served to increase the
hunger for more. The indescribable, shrinking,
despairing tone and gesture with which Ella cried,
"Then I have lost you for my friend." was vividly
present with him. and before he slept that night, or
rather morning, he poured forth on paper all his love,
his aspirations, that could be written. He did not,
as letter-writing heroes generally do, sacrifice a heca-
tomb of note-paper. He knew what he wanted, and

said it in good, terse, downright English, stamped
with so much earnestness and honesty that it would
have been a cold heart, much colder than Ella Rivers's,
that could have read it unmoved. Then, like a sensible man—for in spite of the strong love fit upon
him, and the rather insane line of conduct he had
chosen to adopt, Wilton was a sensible fellow—he set
himself to wait patiently till the following day, which
might bring him a reply, or possibly a meeting with Ella
herself, which he had most urgently entreated. That
she would either write or come he felt sure, and so to
while away the time he kept a half-made appointment
with some of his military friends, and enjoyed a sharp
run over a stiff country with the D——shire hounds,
and dined with the mess afterwards.

He was, however, less composed next day when
no letter reached him from Ella, and no Ella appeared
at the tryst. The next day was stormy, with heavy
showers, and the next was frosty—still no letter ; still
no Ella—and Wilton began to fret, and champ the bit
of imperious circumstance with suppressed fury. If
to-morrow brought no better luck he would endure it
no longer, but make a bold inroad upon the fortress
wherein his love—his proud, delicate darling—was
held in durance vile.

The weather was still bright and clear. A light
frost lay crisp and sparkling on the short herbage and

tufts of broom ; the air was so still, that the rush of
the river, as it chafed against the big black stones
opposing its progress, could be heard at a considerable distance past the cairn, where a path very little
frequented branched off to a remote hamlet over the
wooded hill behind Glenraven. The low-lying country
towards Monkscleugh lay mapped out in the rarefied
air, which diminished distance and gave wondrous
distinctness to all outlines. A delicious winter's day ;
all sounds mellowed to a sort of metallic music by
the peculiar state of the atmosphere. But Wilton
was in no mood to enjoy the beauties of nature. He
was feverish with impatience as he walked to and fro
behind the friendly shelter of the cairn, and noticed,
in the odd, mechanical way with which the mind at
certain crises seems excited into a species of double
action, and while absorbed by the great motive can
yet take in and imprint indelibly upon its tablets all
the minute details of surrounding objects. He saw
the picturesque roughness of a prostrate tree ; he
watched the shadow of the cairn stealing gradually
further eastward ; he noticed a little robin perching
on a twig, that seemed to look at him without apprehension ; he gazed at a couple of ragged, miserable
goats who were feeding at a little distance, occasionally lifting up their heads to bleat at each other.
Years after he could have described the position of

these objects, though at the moment he was scarce conscious of them. "Ten minutes to three! If she is not here in ten minutes, I will walk on to Brosedale and find out why," he muttered to himself, as he walked away once more toward the hill. When he turned he saw a slight figure, wrapped in a dark green plaid, standing beside the tree, in the place he had just quitted. Then—impatience, and doubt, and anger all swept away in a flood of delight—he sprang to meet her.

"At last! I thought you would never come. And yet how good of you to grant my request. I have lived two years since I spoke to you."

Ella smiled and colored, then turned very pale, and gently, but firmly, drew away the hand he had taken—looking on the ground all the time. "I could not come before," she said, in a low, unsteady voice. "To-day Sir Peter has taken Donald with him to D——." A pause. "I am afraid you thought me rude—unkind—but I scarcely understood you. I—" She stopped abruptly.

"Do you understand me now?" asked Wilton, gravely, coming close to her, and resting one foot only on the fallen tree, while he bent to look into the sweet, pale face. "Have you read my letter?"

"Yes; many times, It has infinitely astonished me."

" Why ? "

" That you should ask so great a stranger to share your life—your name. To be with you always—till death. Is it not unwise, hasty ? "

" Many—most people would say so, who were not in love. I cannot reason or argue about it. I only know that I cannot face the idea of life without you. Nor shall anything turn me from my determination to win you, except your own distinct rejection."

" Is it possible you feel all this—and for me ? " exclaimed Ella, stepping back and raising her great, deep, blue, wondering eyes to his.

" I loved you from the hour we first met," said Wilton, passionately. " For God's sake ! do not speak so coldly. Are you utterly indifferent to me ? or have you met some one you can love better ? "

" Neither," she replied, still looking earnestly at him. " I never loved any one. I have often thought of loving, and feared it ! it is so solemn. But how could I love you ? I have always liked to meet you and speak to you, still I scarcely know you ; and though to me such things are folly, I know that to you and to your class there seems a great gulf fixed between us—a gulf I never dreamed you would span."

" I do not care what the gulf, what the obstacle," cried Wilton, again possessing himself of her hand ; " I only know that no woman was ever before neces-

sary to my existence ; high or low, you are my queen !
Do not think I should have dared to express my feel
ings so soon, but for the enormous difficulty of seeing
you—of meeting you. Then I feared that you might
drift away from me. I am not wanting in pluck ; but,
by heaven ! I never was in such a fright in my life as
the other night when I began to speak to you."

A sweet smile stole round Ella's lips and sparkled
in her eyes as he spoke. " Ah ! you are not going
to be inexorable," he continued, watching with delight
this favorable symptom ; " if you are heart-whole I do
not quite despair."

" Colonel Wilton," she replied, again drawing away
her hand, " take care you are not acting on a mere
impulse."

" You speak as if I were a thoughtless, inexperienced boy," he interrupted, impatiently. " You forget
that I was almost a man when you were born ; and as
to reflecting, I have never ceased reflecting since I
met you. Believe me, I have thought of everything
possible and impossible, and the result is you must be
my wife, unless you have some insuperable objection."

" Oh, let me speak to you," she exclaimed, clasping her hands imploringly ; " speak out all my mind,
and do not be offended, or misinterpret me."

" I will listen to every syllable, and stand any
amount of lecturing you choose to bestow ; but let us

walk on toward the hill; you will take cold standing
here."

They moved on accordingly, Ella speaking with
great, though controlled, animation—sometimes stopping to enforce her words with slight, eloquent gestures. Wilton's heart in his eyes, listening with his
whole soul, slowly and meditatively pulling out his
long moustaches.

"Nature to nature," continued Ella. "I know I
am not unworthy of you, even if you are all you seem.
But are you quite sure you will always see as clearly
through the outside of things as you do now? Ah! I
have heard and read such sad, terrible stories of
change, and vain regret for what was irremediable,
that I tremble at the thought of what you might bring
upon us both. Mind to mind, heart to heart, we are
equals; but the accidents of our condition—just look
at the difference between them. I am the veriest
thistledown of insignificance. I scarce know who I
am myself; and might not the day come when you
will regret having sacrificed your future to a fancy, a
whim? You might be too generous to say so, but do
you think I should not know it? If I married you I
would love you, and if I loved you there would not be
a shadow on your heart, nor a variation in your mood
that I should not divine. Do not ask me to love you.

I fear it! I am quiet now; my life is not very sunny, but it is free from absolute pain. Be wise."

"I am wise," interrupted Wilton; "most wise in my resolution to let nothing turn me from my purpose; and Ella—for I must speak to you as I think of you—do not suppose I am offering you a very brilliant lot when I implore you to be my wife. I am but indifferently off as a simple gentleman, and will be positively poor when I have higher rank. Still, if you will trust me—if you will love me—life may be very delicious. All that you have said only makes me more eager to call you my own. I am not afraid of changing. I have always been true to my friends—why not to my love? It is true that you must take me somewhat on my own recommendation; but is there no instinctive feeling in your heart that recognizes the sincerity of mine? I have listened to all you have said, and simply repeat—Will you be my wife, if you are free to be so?"

"I will answer frankly, yes. Oh, stay, stay! *If* after six months' absence you return and repeat the question—"

"Six months' absence! You are not speaking seriously! Do you think I should consent to such banishment?"

"You must, Colonel Wilton, both for your own sake and mine. I must be sure that the feelings you

think so deep will stand some test ; you ought to
prove your real need of me by absence, by steeping
yourself in the society of your own class—the women
of your own class.   I have a right to ask this."

" By heaven ! " cried Wilton, " you are utterly cold
and indifferent, or you would not put me to so cruel a
proof.'

Ella was silent, and tears stood in her eyes, while
Wilton went on.   " Think of six months ! six months
swept clean off the few years of youth and love and
happiness we have before us !   It is reckless waste !
Hear me in turn ; give up this purgatory ! go back to
your friendly landlady.   I will meet you in London ;
in three or four weeks at the farthest we shall be man
and wife.   I have more than three months' leave un-
expired ; we will go away to Italy, or the south of
France.   Ella ! I feel half-mad at the idea of such a
heaven.   Why do you not feel as I do ? "

" No, I must not, I will not," said she, turning very
pale, and trembling excessively, but letting him hold
her hand in both his.   " I must insist upon your sub-
mitting to the test of absence, in justice to me."

In vain Wilton implored and almost raged ; she
was evidently much shaken and disturbed, but still
immovable.   The utmost Wilton could win was the
shortening his time of probation to three months, during which time he was not to write nor expect her to

write. If, at the expiration of that period, he claimed
her, she would be his. If he changed, he was simply
to let the tryst go by unnoticed. The settlement of
these preliminaries brought them very near the entrance of the Brosedale plantations, whither Ella had
resolutely bent her steps. Finding his eloquence of
no avail, Wilton was rather moodily silent.

"You are angry; you think me unkind," said
Ella, softly; "but however you decide you will yet
thank me."

"You do not feel as I do."

"Perhaps not; yet do not think that it costs me
nothing to say good-by. You always cheered me. I
used to look for you when I came out to walk, and
when you used to come and see Donald I always felt
less alone."

"If you feel all this, why do you banish me?"

"Because it is wisest and kindest; and now good-
by. Yes; do go! I want to be back in time to grow
composed before Donald returns."

"Dearest, you look awfully pale. I ought not to
keep you; and yet I cannot part with you." He drew
her to him most tenderly, irresistibly impelled to
breathe his adieu on her lips.

"No, no," she exclaimed, drawing back. "I dare
not kiss you; a kiss to me would be a marriage bond;

do not ask it; do not hold me." He felt how she trembled, and he released her.

"One day, Ella, you will perhaps know how much I must love to obey you. So it must be good-by?"

"Yes; and remember you leave me perfectly free. I say it with no arrogance or want of feeling, but if you do not return, I shall not break my heart. I shall rather rejoice that we have escaped a great mistake— a terrible sorrow—but if you do come back—" A soft blush stole over her cheek—a bright smile. Wilton gazed at her, waiting eagerly for the next words, but they did not come. "Whatever happens," she resumed, "I shall always remember with pleasure, with respect, that for once you rose above the conventional gentleman into a natural, true man." She gave him her hand for a moment, then, drawing it away from his passionate kisses, disappeared in the fast increasing gloom of evening among the plantations.

CHAPTER VIII.

A BRIGHT, blustering March morning was shining, with a cold glitter over the square of the well-known B—— Barracks, in that pleasant, rackety capital, Dublin, nearly three months after the interview last recorded. Parade had just been dismissed, and the officers of the second battalion —th Rifles had dispersed to their various occupations or engagements, with the exception of a small group which gathered round an attractive fire in the mess-room, and discussed the military and club gossip of the hour.

"Will you stay for the —th Dragoons' ball, on Thursday, Wilton?" said one of the younger men to our friend, who was reading a London paper, and dressed in mufti, evidently a guest.

"And for St. Paddy's on the 17th?" asked the colonel. "It's a dazzling scene, and no end of fun."

"I promised to dine with the mess of the —th Dragoons to-night," returned Wilton; "and I think I should like to see their ball; but I must be in Scotland before the 17th, so must forego the humors of St. Patrick's. I see, colonel, my battalion was not to

embark until the 25th of February. They cannot
reach England for another month. I have a great
mind to exchange into the regiment that is gone out
to relieve them. I do not like soldiering in England
—there is always work to be done in India."

The colonel elevated his brows.

"My dear fellow, you are desperately energetic.
I should have thought that, with your prospects, you
had done work enough."

"My prospects have nothing to do with it. I
suppose there would be no difficulty in the matter?"
continued Wilton, reflectively, more to himself than
to his listener.

"Difficulty! none whatever. The fighting is over,
so no one will be afraid to stay at home ; and I fancy
there is a very uncomfortable transition-state before
the Anglo-Indian world."

"I shall ask for extension of leave ; I don't fancy
joining the depot."

"How long is Moncrief to be away?"

"He has three weeks' leave—urgent private
affairs. I am sure to see him in town, though I shall
only pass through," remarked Wilton, and relapsed
into silence, scarcely hearing the arguments of his
companion, who proved to demonstration that Wilton
would be a fool to make any exchange, except, indeed,

he could get a chance of returning to his old friends of the second battalion.

Ralph Wilton was looking thinner and graver than formerly, and there was an expression of anxiety and irritation in his keen bold eyes. While the colonel argued, an orderly approached with letters, which his officer took, and, glancing at the addresses, handed two or three to Wilton. "This is from Moncrief," said he, opening an envelope directed in a remarkably stiff, legible hand—"forwarded from Athgarven. He is annoyed at missing me, and—" Here he stopped, and read on, with knit brows and fixed attention, then let the hand which held the letter drop, and stood wrapped in thought.

"No bad news?" asked the colonel.

"Yes—no," he returned, absently. "My dear colonel, I must leave you to-day. I must go up to town by this evening's mail."

"This is very sudden. Can't you manage a day or two more? Why, you have only been three weeks with us."

A few words from Wilton convinced his friend and host that, although indisposed to give a reason for his sudden move, its necessity was imperative.

The passage in Major Moncrief's letter which had moved Wilton was as follows :

"Town is very full ; the club brimming over ; din-

ners going a-begging—and, talking of dinners, I met
our Monkscleugh acquaintance, Lady Fergusson, in
Regent Street, yesterday. She was in deep mourning; it seems that unfortunate son and heir died
about a month ago. Sir Peter is in great grief; the
establishment at Brosedale broken up, and the whole
family *en route* for Germany. I wonder what has
become of the pretty lassie you picked up in the
snow! I was always afraid of your getting into some
mess with her; but you have more sense than I gave
you credit for."

The Brosedale establishment broken up! and not
a line—not a word—from Ella. Where had she
gone? Did she wish to avoid him? In four days
more the three months' absence prescribed by Ella
would have expired, and now he was thrown off the
scent. Had she sought and found any new employ-
ment? If in her heart she distrusted his constancy
as much as she professed, she might have done so; or
had she returned to that London landlady whom she
had described on the memorable occasion of the
snow-storm? Hold! he had noted the address somewhere. This led to a vehement search among his
papers and memoranda; but in vain. Then he sat
down and thought intensely. Kershaw?—yes, that
was the name of the woman; and Gothic Villa the
name of the house at Kensington; but the street,

that he could not recall ; nevertheless, he would not
leave a corner of the "old court suburb" unexplored.
With this resolution he started on his journey—the
mere movement raised his spirits and invigorated
him ; anything was better than the silence and endur-
ance of the last three months.

He had parted with Ella Rivers in a mood curiously compounded of love, anger, slightly-mortified
vanity, but deep admiration.   He felt that she had a
right to demand some test of a passion so sudden ;
and, without words, her grave candor had impressed
upon him the conviction that, in asking her to share
his life, he asked quite as much as he offered—a conviction not always clear to men, even when in love.
Then the respect which her self-control, her noble
simplicity, imposed upon him, deepened and elevated
the character of his affection.   Above all, she was
still to be won.   She had allowed him to hope ; but he
dared not flatter himself that she loved him—and
how wonderfully he yearned for her love !—he was
astonished at it himself.   All life seemed empty and
colorless without her.   About three weeks after he
had left Glenraven, he had written to let her know
that he had accepted an invitation to Ireland, where
he intended to make some stay and visit his former
brother-officers, seizing gladly the excuse afforded by

this change of locality; but he had quickly received the following reply:

"You must faithfully keep the promise you have given. Do not in any way seek me for three or four months. Meantime, I am well and not unhappy. Whether we meet again or not, I shall ever think of you kindly. May the good God guide us to what is happiest and best for both!

"Always your friend,
"ELLA RIVERS."

The small, straight, firm writing was kissed again and again, even while he chafed against her firmness. This touch of the true magnet had drawn all the atoms of romance, of nobility, of perception of spiritual and intellectual light, which lay scattered, not sparingly, among the coarser material of the man, into symmetrical circles converging to one centre. He was softened and strengthened. He resolved to obey Ella to the letter; and his brother-officers noticed that Wilton was much more ready for balls and dinners and luncheon-parties than formerly; for his character had been rather that of a "reserved, quiet fellow, with a devil of a temper when roused." He was, nevertheless, a favorite, as straightforward, plucky men, who never "shirk their fences" in any sense, generally are. The neighborhood, too, where Wilton's visit was made, was unusually wealthy and aristocratic

for Ireland, so that he had ample opportunities for
"steeping" himself in the society of people of his own
class. The result, however, was that the impression
he had received sank deeper and more abidingly as
time went on. And now, when this fresh difficulty
arose, he sprang forward upon the search with all the
eagerness of a sleuth-hound suddenly released from his
chain.

It was in the dim gray of a cold, drizzling morning
that Wilton reached Morley's Hotel. After a bath
and breakfast, he sallied forth, in search of Moncrief.
During his long night-journey he had taken counsel
with himself as to how he should proceed. He would
learn Lady Fergusson's present address, and endeavor
to ascertain from her what had become of Ella. How
he was to accomplish this without rousing her ladyship's suspicions, he would leave to the inspiration of
the moment; for it was no part of his scheme to
unmask his movements until he could really fix his
plans. This could not be done till he had seen Ella
and received a renewal of her promise; or—terrible
alternative—been rejected and overthrown! Her
unaccountable silence was cruel, unfeeling, and a
clear breach of faith. Why had she not written to
announce so material a change of circumstances?
Had any of the pestilent political crew that used to
surround her father started up to exercise an evil

influence? The idea fired him with indignation. He had so delighted in thinking of her as his alone—a hidden jewel, the lustre and value and beauty of which were for him only! Meditating thus, he reached the frugal major's lodgings, as he did not wish at present to confront the publicity of a club. But his friend had not yet emerged from the privacy of his chamber, and there was only a dingy back-parlor, a sort of general waiting-room, into which he could be shown. Wilton therefore wrote hastily on his card, "What is Lady Fergusson's address in town?" and sent it up to Moncrief; receiving it back again in a few minutes, with this inscription on the reverse; "Claridge's; but I think they are gone. Dine with me to-day at the club—seven, sharp."

Leaving word that he could not dine with Major Moncrief, Wilton left the house in a state of irritability and depression, and bent his steps to Claridge's; early as it was, he might at least make inquiries there. A yawning porter, who was sweeping the hall, called a waiter, who informed him that "Sir Peter and Lady Fergusson, the Misses Saville and suite," had started for Paris the day before.

"And suite!" echoed Wilton; "I suppose that includes the governess?"

"Yes, sir; there was a lady as went with the

youngest lady in one of the hotel broughams; she
was the governess."

"Was she a tall, thin lady, with spectacles?"

"Just so, sir."

"No other lady with them?"

"No, sir—none."

Nothing more to be learned there! He was quite
afloat. No clue to the girl who he had hoped would
be, two days hence, his affianced bride, beyond the
vague address, "Mrs. Kershaw, Gothic Villa, Kensington." He made his way slowly into Piccadilly
and hailed a hansom. Kensington must be the scene
of his research, and the sooner he plunged into it the
better.

How to begin occupied his thoughts as he bowled
along. Shops, police, and postmen, seemed the most
likely sources of information; failing these, he must
manage to communicate with Miss Walker, who would
certainly know Ella's whereabouts. However, he had
great faith in himself; it was not the first time he had
to hunt up a faint track, though the difficulties were of
a far different character.

"Here we are! Where to now, sir?" cried Cab-
by, through the hole at the top.

"Oh! a—the nearest butcher's," said Wilton.
"Bread and meat and tea," he reflected, "the hum-
blest landlady must require;" and, proud of his own

reasoning powers, he dismissed the cab, never remembering—probably not knowing—the ready-money system, which, paying the amount and carrying off the article, "leaves not a wrack behind."

The important and substantial butcher, struck by the lordly bearing of his interrogator, condescended to repeat the words "Gothic Villa" in several keys, as though the reiteration would evoke knowledge, but ended with, "Can't say I know any such place, sir.— Here, Smith"—to a blue-gowned assistant, with rolled-up sleeves, who was adding "one leg more" to an artistically arranged fringe of legs of mutton which adorned the cornice—"do you know anything of 'Mrs. Kershaw, Gothic Villa?'"

"Kershaw!" replied the man, pausing—"I seems as if I do, and yet I don't."

At this maddening reply, Wilton felt disposed to collar him and rouse his memory by a sound shaking.

"The person I want lets lodgings; and is, I think, elderly."

"No, I don't," repeated the butcher's assistant. "I know Gothic 'all."

"Ay," struck in the master, "and Gothic 'Ouse and Gothic Lodge, but no willar. I know the place well, sir, and I don't think there is a Gothic Willer in it. P'r'aps it's lodge, not willer, you are looking for?"

" Then who lives at these other Gothics ? "

" Oh, Mr. Reynolds, the great ironmonger, has the 'all; and the honorable Mrs. Croker lives at the lodge."

" Well, neither of these names can possibly be converted into Kershaw. I am sorry I troubled you."

" No trouble at all, sir."

Patiently, though anxiously, Wilton went from butcher to baker, from baker to butterman, from butterman to milkshop, until he suddenly exclaimed at his own stupidity, as his eye was caught by a conspicuous brass plate bearing the inscription, " Mr. Mayers, Gas-Inspector." " By Jove ! " cried Wilton, aloud, " that is the fellow to know every house in the parish. Why did I not think of a gas-inspector before ? "

He rang, and a smart young woman appeared at the door in a few moments.

In his uncertainty whether he was speaking to the wife or the handmaid of Mayers, Wilton politely raised his hat, and asked if he could see the master of the house.

" I am very sorry, sir, he is out, and will not be here till tea-time."

" And when will that be ? " asked the anxious querist, smiling blandly.

"Oh, not till half-past five. Could I give any message?" replied the lady, much impressed by the grand air and chivalrous courtesy of her interlocutor.

"I am afraid I must trouble Mr. Mayers myself. I shall not detain him beyond a moment or two, if he will be so good as to see me about half-past five."

"Yes, sir; he will be in then and very happy to see you."

"Perhaps you happen to know where Gothic Villa is in this neighborhood. I am looking for a Mrs. Kershaw, Gothic Villa."

"Kershaw? Gothic Villa? No, indeed, I do not. I have very few acquaintances here; you see people are rather mixed in Kensington."

"I will not keep you standing—at five-thirty, then," returned Wilton, raising his hat, and smiling as he said to himself, "Madame the gas-inspectress is exclusive. Such caricatures ought to cure the follies they travesty." He looked at his watch. Two hours and a half to spare. What should he do? Make any further search, or rely on the gas-inspector? Yes; he would be sure to know. So, after a moment's thought, he again called a hansom, and rattled back to the club; but Major Moncrief was not there. Hastily scribbling an invitation to breakfast next day, he went on to his hotel to snatch a mouthful of luncheon or dinner, or both, for he still hoped to spend the re-

mainder of the evening exchanging vows, explanations
—perhaps kisses—with Ella Rivers.   He had by some
unreasonable process of thought convinced himself
that she could have taken refuge in no other haven
than the somewhat unromantic dwelling of Mrs.
Kershaw.

As the half-hour struck, Wilton rang again at the
gas-inspector's house.   He was received by the same
lady most graciously, and ushered into an oppressively
smart front parlor, profusely decorated with anti-ma-
cassars, and mats, and table covers.

"Mr. Mayers will be here directly; he has only
just come in.   What a disagreeable day it has been—
drizzle, drizzle, the whole time ! I couldn't venture out,"
simpered Mrs. Mayers, who was disposed to improve
the occasion by a little conversation with her "stylish
visitor," as she described him to her husband.   Wilton
assented rather absently, and then, to his great relief,
Mr. Mayers came in.   After a few words of apology,
Wilton put the oft-repeated question.

"Kershaw, Gothic Villa ? " repeated Mr. Mayers,
meditating.   "Yes, of course, I know wellnigh every
house ; and it so happened I was at Mrs. Kershaw's
a week or ten days back.   Why, it is in H—— Street,
not far from Holland Park.   You must turn right
from this, then first to your right, and third to the

left. Gothic Villa is down the end of the street, opposite a dead wall."

With many thanks and apologies, Wilton bowed himself out, and walked away rapidly, his heart beating high at the idea of the meeting so near at hand.

Gothic Villa was not a lively residence ; and, what was worse, it looked untidy. The box borders looked as if lately trodden down in patches ; the bell was broken, and the gate hung awry, refusing, after the fashion of crooked things, to do one thing or the other —to open wide or shut close. Wilton felt unutterably shocked at the melancholy, sordid aspect of the place. The bell being broken, he felt at a loss how to summon the garrison ; but while he hesitated, two little girls, in short frocks, dingy stockings, and battered hats, came up bowling their hoops, and began rattling their hoop-sticks noisily against the railings, whereupon the front-door was flung suddenly wide open, and a grimy servant began to shout some objurgations to the juveniles.

"Pray, does Mrs. Kershaw live here?" asked Wilton, advancing to the door.

" No ; there's no such name here."

For a moment Wilton felt annihilated.

" She used to live here ? "

" P'r'aps so ; we've not been here above a week, and I wish we was out of it."

"And do you know where Mrs. Kershaw is gone?"

"No, that I don't."

After a little talking, she suggested that "missus" might know; but that potentate, on being appealed to, confessed ignorance, stating, however, that "master" might know; but "master" was absent, and would not be back till to-morrow morning. More Wilton could not extract; and he most reluctantly left the long-sought villa, informing the inmates that he would call next day, hoping that "master" might be able to supply the desired information.

Still, with unshaken perseverance, Wilton lingered about. He stopped the postman, but he had had no letter since the new people moved in for Mrs. Kershaw. She had very few letters at any time—still she had some. There was another postman that took the noonday delivery, he might know. When did he go round? Oh, from twelve to twelve-thirty. He might know, and he mightn't. Addresses were not given to the letter-carriers, but left at the district office.

"Ah! then I may probably find this Mrs. Kershaw's whereabouts at the post-office?"

"No, no, sir," said the man; "they won't give you no addresses at the office, and the letters is sent on to the district where the party has moved; so it's a chance if any of us knows."

"At any rate, I shall be here to-morrow to meet

the twelve o'clock man ; meantime I am obliged to you."

So saying, Wilton deposited a judicious tip in the carrier's willing hand, and made for the main road, hoping that a favorable report of him would be given to the other carrier, and predispose him to be communicative.

It was long before Wilton forgot the oppressive monotony of that evening. He could not bring himself to seek out Moncrief. He would have him at breakfast, and that was bad enough. He strolled into the Adelphi, and felt savage at the pathos of the play, and the fun of the afterpiece. He left before it was finished, and returned to the coffee-room. He tried to sketch out an advertisement addressed to Mrs. Kershaw, but intended for Ella. He vexed himself with all kinds of conjectures, and finally retired, hoping for oblivion in sleep, which did not come for some weary hours ; and his last waking thought was that tomorrow would be the 19th of March, the day of the tryst, which he had so often pictured to himself. And here he was in total ignorance of Ella's dwelling—not a step nearer to the desired interview. The following day was not much brighter than the one just described, and Wilton rose with an unspeakable loathing for breakfast and Moncrief—especially Moncrief.

However, both had to be endured. The major was

considerably puzzled by his entertainer's preoccupation and testiness. Every subject seemed distasteful, every person more or less offensive.

"What's come to you, lad?" asked the old soldier. "Are you in debt again? I thought you had left that class of troubles behind you; and you seem to have been quiet and steady enough of late."

"No, I am not in debt."

"Well, I do not think you are in love; and love, or money, is at the bottom of most troubles—eh?"

An inaudible muttering was the only reply.

"A — idiot?" repeated the major, thinking he caught the sound. "No, by no means. I never said so, though there have been times when I was afraid you would act like one. Have you seen the viscount?"

"No."

"I suppose you are going to call on him?"

"No, I am not."

"Then you are rather an idiot. Why will you throw away fortune?"

"I am not throwing it away. He is out of town."

"Why don't you go and pay him a visit?"

"I cannot; he has not asked me."

"Not asked you—bosh!—"

"Moncrief," interrupted Wilton, "will you take some more kidney, or ham, or coffee, or anything?"

" No, thank you ; I have breakfasted well."

" Then go, will you ? like a good fellow. You are partly right. I am in a pickle. You shall know all about it one of these days, but I cannot tell you just now. I have an appointment at—that is, I must be at Kensington at twelve."

" At twelve ! Bless my soul, man, it is scarcely half-past ten now."

CHAPTER IX.

THE afternoon of the same day was lowering, bleak, and drear, as a young girl, in a long black dress fitting close to her slight figure, and relieved at throat and wrists by a plaiting of white crape, entered a small sitting-room at the back of one of a row of brand-new residences in the cardboard, Tudor style, inlaid with colored bricks, and further relieved by oriel windows.

The young lady carried a cup full of violets, and set it upon a table which had been moved into the window. It was crowded with materials for water-color drawing. A very graceful design suited to a portfolio lay partly colored where the light fell strongest.

The young lady, or rather Ella Rivers, stood looking at her work for a few minutes, and then sitting down, with a deep sigh, took up her brush, first bending lovingly over the violets until her face touched them.

She was exceedingly pale—the pallor of thought and sorrow. Her eyes, which looked larger than they used—perhaps because she had grown thinner—had a weary, wistful expression, which gave pathos to the quiet sadness of her face and figure. The last month had tried her sorely. The sudden, fatal illness of Donald had caused her immense bodily fatigue and real sorrow. She had grown to love the afflicted, wayward boy, even more than she knew; and he could not bear her out of his sight, finally breathing his last in her arms. Then, not understanding the terms which existed between Wilton and the Fergusson family, Ella never doubted that he was aware from the first of poor Sir Peter's bereavement and the consequent removal of the family. His silence under such circumstances, the absence of any attempt to seek her out, was, to her, conclusive evidence that his sudden, violent affection for herself had passed away. Arriving at this conviction showed her how fondly, although unconsciously, she had hoped for his constancy. When Wilton astonished and agitated her by his unexpected avowal, she had most truly told him that she did not love him, that his truth or constancy was not essential to her happiness. His frank kindness, and the interest he had shown in her art and her conversation, had touched and diverted her. Feeling keenly the insurmountable barrier of caste, which her reason scornfully resented, the possibility of a man of his grade being her lover never crossed her mind. Moreover,

the habits of her life accustomed her to men as com-
panions, as friends, almost as playfellows, but never as
lovers. Wilton was therefore to her at first an agreeable, intelligent, though mistaken man, blinded to the
great truths of his age by his position and his profession, but who, under higher direction, might have been
worthy the friendship of her father, Diego, and the
rest of the exalted society who passed their lives pro-
pagating theories of political perfection and escaping
the police.

After the wonderful interview by the cairn, where
he had shown that, although past the boy-lover period,
he was ready to cast all consideration for rank and
riches to the winds for her sake, she had estimated
him very differently. From his first words of love she
shrunk with an agony she could not express, so certain
was she that they must mean insult; but when his
letter told her the depth and sincerity of his affection,
and she listened to the magic of his earnest pleading,
she felt bewildered and almost frightened at the ardor
of the feeling she had evoked. She could not quite
believe him. She trembled at the idea of his hurrying
into the irrevocable, which he might afterward regret ;
and the more she felt her heart inclined to yield, the
more resolutely she held to her determination, for both
their sakes, to test the reality of his affection.

But when he was gone, when she was left alone

with the memory of his persuasive voice—of his bold brown eyes, softened into tenderness—of the passion which glowed through the earnest respect of his manner—whatever of indifference she had felt or assumed in their interview fast faded away, or rather warmed into real interest, and trembling, half-fearful liking. Then the question of his constancy assumed an absorbing importance. The perpetual struggle in her mind to resist the delightful suggestions of hope kept the subject constantly before her; and the bitterest trial she had ever known was the gradual fading away of the hopes that had formed themselves in spite of her, when week after week slipped past and no tidings reached her from Ralph Wilton. Of course he knew that she must leave Brosedale, and must also know that under no circumstances would she take the first step toward the renewal of their intercourse.

Working round this dreary circle of thought, she sat motionless, pencil in hand, too absorbed to notice the entrance of a woman of a certain age, who by her costume evidently aimed at the higher appellation of a lady. She wore a handsome plum-colored silk, a tint which appears to be the especial favorite of publicans' wives and aspiring landladies. Her head—a high, narrow, self-asserting sort of head—was perched on a long, thin neck, and adorned with a scanty screw of hair on the top, secured by a high tortoise-shell comb, while the front tresses were disposed in short, wiry ringlets. painfully suggestive of steel springs, and carefully regulated by ancient contrivances called side-combs. These locks vibrated when she moved; and as her walk was a succession of jerky sinkings and risings, the ringlets had an active time of it. Her features were regular and good, but somewhat neutralized by a faint expression of constantly turning up her nose, which was anything but *retroussé*, as if in contemptuous indignation at the futile efforts of the world in general to take her in. This personage paused as she was half across the little room, and looked very sharply at its occupant's profile, which was turned to her.

"Anyways, you ain't breaking your heart with hard work," she exclaimed, in a tone which would have been painfully acute but for a slight indistinctness caused by a melancholy gap where pearly front teeth ought to have been.

Ella started at her voice, and a large tear, which some time, unknown to her, had hung upon her eyelashes, fell upon the edge of her paper. She looked at it dismayed; half an inch nearer, and it would have played havoc with her colors. She hastily placed her handkerchief on the fatal spot, and, turning toward the speaker, said, absently : "Working ! Yes,

Mrs. Kershaw; I am succeeding tolerably with this design; I am quite interested in it."

"And that is the reason you are crying over it —eh?"

"Crying! Oh, no"—smiling a little sadly—"I am not crying."

"Something very like it, then," said Mrs. Kershaw, advancing to the table and looking critically at Ella's work. "It's a queer thing," she remarked, with high-toned candor. "What is it for?"

"Oh, the cover of a book, or—the back of a portfolio."

"Well, I suppose it's my ignorance; but I can't see the beauty of it. Why, there's dozens and dozens of things just like that ready printed in all the shops; and you don't suppose hand-work can hold its own with machine-work? Why don't you paint a house, and a tree, and a cow—something sensible-like—that would set off a nice, handsome frame? I wouldn't mind buying such a picture myself; my first floor is a trifle naked for want of pictures."

"O Mrs. Kershaw!" exclaimed Ella, smiling, this time more brightly, for she was amused at her friend's notions of art; "I assure you an original design is not to be despised. If I can but find favor with—"

"Ay, that's just it. It would take a heap of bits of pictures to make a living. I must say I think you

was a fool not to look out for something steady right
off, when the ladies as could have recommended you
was here ; this will be hard work and poor work."

"Nevertheless, I am determined to try it," said Ella,
firmly, though sadly. "You cannot tell the imprisonment a great house is to me; besides, you forget poor
Sir Peter Fergusson's generosity. I can afford to
board with you for six or eight months, and then, if
all my efforts to earn my bread by my art fail, I can
still ask Miss Walker's help. I am not in your way,
good friend, am I ?"

"Well, no. I am not that selfish, like many, as
would try to keep you here when it would be better
for you to be away ; but you are not like other girls,
the place is different when you are in it ; and the trifle
you pay is more than the trifle difference you make.
It was about yourself—what is best for you—I was
thinking."

"Do not think of me," returned Ella, placing her
elbow on the table and resting her head on her hand
despondently ; "I am so weary of myself."

"Now there is something come to you quite different from what used to be. And you are that pale
and thin, and don't eat nothing. There's some of
those grandedees " (such was Mrs. Kershaw's pronun-
ciation) "been talking nonsense, and you have been,
and gone, and been fool enough to heed them, in

spite of all the talking to I gave you before you went
to Sir Peter's. They are all alike. If you was a
hangel, with a wing sprouting out of each shoulder,
and as beautiful as—as anythink, the poorest scrap
of a gentleman among them that hadn't as much
gumption as would earn a crust costermongering
would laugh at the notion of putting a ring on your
finger. No, no ; as much love as you like without
that. I knows 'em, the proud, upsetting, lazy lot, I
do ;" and Mrs. Kershaw stopped with a jerk, more
for want of breath than lack of matter.

"You need not distress yourself," returned Ella,
with a smile of quiet scorn. "No one insulted me at
Brosedale ; and I *did* keep your good advice in mind.
I am depressed, nor can you wonder at it when you
think of the sad scenes I went through with poor
Donald."

"Well, well, anyhow you won't open your mind to
me, though I fancy I am your best friend, and your
only friend into the bargain, though I say it as
shouldn't," retorted Mrs. Kershaw, with some asperity.

"You are, indeed," said Ella, sweetly. "So
instead of quarelling with me for not telling you a romantic tale, tell me some of your own affairs ; any
one about the rooms yet ?"

"I believe," said Mrs. Kershaw, a shade less
severely—"I believe I'm let."

14

This startling announcement did not in the least move Miss Rivers from her gravity; she merely observed, sympathetically, "I am very glad."

"This morning, when you was out, a lady and gentleman called, and looked at the rooms, and made rather a stiff bargain. They said they would call again; but the gentleman gave me his card, and that looked like business."

"I suppose so. I went over to Kensington this morning to see the postman. I thought it was as well to tell him our new address, in case there might be a letter for me."

"A letter for you!" repeated Mrs. Kershaw, in a sharp key, with a sudden nod that set her ringlets dancing. "I thought Miss Walker knew we was moved."

"She does; still it is possible some old friend—"

"Hoh!" said Mrs. Kershaw, ironically. "Are you sure it ain't a new friend—a Scotch friend? I know I haven't no right to ask, but—"

"Ah, suspicious one!" interrupted Ella, laughing. "If none of my father's old friends seek me out, no one else will."

"There's the front-door bell!" cried Mrs. Kershaw, excitedly; "that's the lady and gent come back about my first floor"—a pause ensued, a rapid but heavy tread, and the opening of the door was heard.

The next moment that of the room in which they were was flung violently open, and the "girl" announced a "gentleman for Miss Rivers."

Whereupon a tall figure seemed to fill up the door-way, and for a moment Ella felt dizzy and blinded with astonishment, with mingled joy and terror, as Colonel Wilton entered and stood still.

"Hoh!" said Mrs. Kershaw; "do you know this gentleman, or is he after the apartments?"

"I know him. I—" faltered Ella.

"Hoh!" again said Mrs. Kershaw, and, turning back, walked straight out of the room with dignity.

Wilton closed the door after her, and, advancing to the agitated girl, exclaimed, with a tinge of sternness, "Ella, have you hid from me purposely?"

"Hid from you? No; you knew where to find me when poor Donald died."

"Which I first heard of in Ireland two days ago."

"Two days ago!" faltered Ella, the truth dawning on her. "I thought you would have known of it directly. I thought you did not write because you did not wish to see me again. I—oh, listen to me, understand me!" clasping her hand with a restrained eagerness very impressive—"do not think I would willingly have caused you the slightest uneasiness from any petty idea of standing on my dignity; but, indeed, I was puzzled what to do, and then believing, as I did, that you must have been informed of Donald's death and the breaking up of Sir Peter's establishment, I concluded that you had changed your plans—your views—your—oh, I could not write to you! Do you not see I could not?"

"I can only repeat that two days ago I did not know of that poor boy's death. And, but for a few words in a letter from Moncrief, I should have started for Monkscleugh to keep the tryst. Now, Ella, are you glad to see me? do you believe me?"—as he spoke Wilton took both her hands, and looked eagerly into the eyes so frankly, but gravely, raised to his.

"I do believe you," said Ella, trying to speak steadily, and striving to hold back the tears that would well up, to suppress the wild throbbing of the heart which visibly heaved her bosom, to be calm, and mistress of herself in this crisis; but it was more than even her brave spirit could accomplish; the sudden change from darkness to light, from isolation to companionship, was too overwhelming; and yet she would not show the shattered condition of her forces. "I am glad to see you"—her lip quivered, great unshed tears, brimming over, hung sparkling on her long lashes as she spoke; and Wilton, gazing at the sweet face and slight, graceful figure, felt in his inmost soul the pathos of her controlled emotion.

"By Heaven, Ella! you are not indifferent to

me," he exclaimed. Drawing her to him, he raised
her hands to clasp his neck ; and, folding his arms
round her, ' pressed her passionately to his heart.
" My love, my life ! why do you distrust me ? Give
me your heart ! give me yourself. Are you ready to
fulfil your more than half promise ? I have kept the
tryst. I have submitted to the test you have imposed ; and now, what further barrier is there between
me and happiness ? Do you love me, Ella ? Will
you love me ? "

She did not attempt to move. She leaned against
him, silently, trembling very much ; at length she
sighed deeply.

" If you are quite sure of yourself," she almost
whispered, " and not afraid of linking yourself with so
isolated a creature as I am, I am ready to keep my
word, as you have kept yours ! "

" And you love me ? " asked Wilton, bending over
her, hungering for her assurance.

She extricated herself gently from him, still leaving
her hand in his.

" I will love you," she replied, looking away, and
speaking thoughtfully. Then, suddenly turning, and
meeting his eyes with a grand frankness, " I *do* love
you," she said, in her sweet, firm tones ; " and I think
you deserve my love ! If you do not, out with love
and life, and everything ! I shall never believe more."

She pressed her hands over her eyes, and for a moment Wilton's passionate longing to cover her mouth, her cheek, her brow, with kisses, was checked by the earnestness, the solemnity of her words; it was but a moment, the next she was in his arms, his lips clinging to hers as though he could never drink enough of their sweetness.

"And how did you find me?" asked Ella, when at last she managed to-withdraw from his embrace, and began to gather her drawing materials together as a diversion from the strange, sweet embarrassment of the new relations existing between them.

Wilton replied by recapitulating the search he had made, up to the miserable night before.

"When I arrived at Gothic Villa this morning," he went on, "I was considerably before the time of the second delivery; but at last I met the postman, and explained myself to him. 'Gothic Villa, Kershaw,' he repeated. 'Now that's curious. Not ten minutes ago I met a young lady what used to be at Gothic Villa, and she wanted to give me her new address, but I told her she must leave it at the district office.' You may guess the questions I put, and how I gathered that the young lady was yourself. He had a confused idea you said your abode was in Belinda Terrace, Notting Hill, and I have been for nearly the last three hours endeavoring to discover it. Finding there was no such place as Belinda Terrace, I tried my luck in Melina Crescent, and, after knocking and ringing at eleven doors, found the right one at last!"

"Then had I walked down the street, instead of meeting the postman at the top of it, I should have met you," said Ella, pausing in her occupation, with her design in her hand.

"Yes; and saved me three hours of torture," exclaimed Wilton. "What have you there? This is a very charming design; quite your own?"

"Yes, quite. Some days ago I took a much smaller one to a shop in —— Street, and the man there gave me two pounds and two shillings for it. Then he asked me to bring him something else, larger and richer, so I have been trying to sketch something better."

"My own darling," said Wilton, taking it from her; "this sort of thing is over now. No more work for you."

"Why not?" she returned. "You say, dear friend, that you are not rich. If I am really to be your comrade through life, why may I not earn some money for us both? Life without work must be very dull."

"When you are my wife, you will see such things are impossible," said Wilton, laying aside the sketch, and drawing her to his side on a little, hard, horsehair, lodging-house sofa. "I have so much to say, so much to urge on you, I hardly know where to begin."

Whereupon he plunged into a rapid statement of his plans, his hopes, his strong conviction that, calmly and dispassionately considered, her position and his own rendered an immediate marriage absolutely and imperatively necessary. She had no one to consult, nor any protector to rely upon save himself, and the sooner he had a legal claim to be her protector the better. As to himself, no one had a right to interfere with him; nevertheless, there was an old man, a relative, who might make himself disagreeable if he had time. After marriage, all objections, interference, or meddlings, would be useless.

"I have a favorite sister to whom I shall write at once," concluded Wilton, "but she is away in Canada. So, dearest, why should we submit to the discomfort of needless delay? I shall have a renewal of leave, but only for a couple of months, part of which must be spent in effecting an exchange into some regiment in India, or going there. You see there will be little left for the honeymoon. What do you say to this day week?"

Wilton felt the hand he held suddenly tighten on his with a quick, startled pressure.

"Yes," he went on; "there is no possible objection. You have been at least three weeks in this parish, which is, I believe, the legal requirement. There is, then, no impediment; and, though it seems very like urging you to take a leap in the dark, you must either trust me altogether or throw me over. We are too peculiarly situated to perform the cold-blooded ceremony of cultivating each other's acquaintance ; we must do that, as I believe all people really do, after rather than before marriage. Besides, I am so desperately afraid of your melting away out of my grasp, as you had nearly done just now, that I am determined not to lose my hold."

"Listen to me," said Ella, drawing away her hand and pressing it to her brow. "You mentioned a relative to whom your marriage might be painful. Do you owe this old man love and respect? I think, if you do, it is hard to those who feel they ought to be considered to find an utter stranger preferred."

"Lord St. George has not the shadow of a claim on my love or respect," returned Wilton, rising and pacing to and fro ; "and if he had it would not influence me. Now that you have really consented to be my wife, nothing save death shall come between us."

There was in his voice, and look, and gesture, such fire and resolution that a sudden sense of being in the presence of something stronger than herself thrilled Ella with a strange fear and pleasure. She closed her eyes, and her hands, that had clasped each other tightly, relaxed as she felt her life had passed from her own keeping into another's. Wilton, who had paused opposite her, saw how deeply she was moved.

"Look at me, Ella!" he exclaimed, taking her hands in his—"look at me! You are too nobly frank to hesitate as to a day sooner or later in the fulfilment of your promise."

She turned to him; and, with a wistful, earnest look straight into his eyes, said, in a low, firm voice:

"So be it! I will keep my word when and where you like."

Two days after, Major Moncrief, who had only seen Wilton once for a few minutes in the interim, awaited him by appointment at Morley's, where they they were to dine.

"Why, what the deuce are you so desperately busy about?" asked the major, as Wilton hastily apologized for not having been ready to receive his friend.

"Oh, I have a hundred things in hand. I have had to 'interview' my lawyer, and then I have been with Box and Brushwood about exchanging into a regiment under orders for India—and—but the rest after dinner."

"Why, what are you up to now?" replied Moncrief, but not in the tone of a man that expects a direct reply.

Dinner passed very agreeably, for Wilton was in

brilliant spirits. Not for many a year had Moncrief see him so bright.

" I believe this is the same room we dined in the day you started for Monkscleugh, and had the smash ? " observed Moncrief, as the waiter, having placed dessert on the table, left the friends together.

" It is," said Wilton, looking round. " 'That is rather curious ; and I remember your saying, ' I must dree my weird.' Well, Moncrief, I have dreed it, and I asked you here to-day to tell you the history, and receive your blessing or malediction, as the case may be."

Setting down his glass of port untasted, the major stared at his friend with an air of dismay and bewilderment.

" Courage, man ! " continued Wilton, laughing at his consternation ; " I am not in debt—only in love, and going to be married on Thursday next."

" To be married ! You—who could not oblige your pleasant relative, Lord St. George, because of your invincible objection to lose your liberty ? "

" Well, the liberty•is gone long ago ; so my only plan is to surrender at discretion, or, rather, without discretion. You remember a young lady we met at Brosedale—the lassie, in short, whom I picked out of the snow ? "

" What ! that pale-faced, dark-eyed little girl—

young Fergusson's companion or drawing-mistress? Why, she was scarcely pretty."

"Just so. Well, I am going to marry her on Thursday. Will you come to the wedding?"

Wilton had poured out a bumper of claret as he spoke, and, with a slight, defiant nod, drank it off.

" By —— ! " exclaimed Moncrief, who did not generally use strong language ; "I am astonished. when did you decide on this preposterous piece of foolery?"

"I put things in train last December, but the date was not decided till two days ago."

"Ha! I thought I smelt a rat just before I left Glenraven ; but I never dreamed of anything so serious. You are the last man I should have accused of such idiotic weakness. Who is this girl?"

"I do not know."

"Who was her father?"

"A political adventurer, I believe; but I really do not know."

"Who are her friends?"

"She has none."

" And, my God! Wilton, are you going to link yourself for life to a woman you know nothing about —who may have a murderer for her father and a harlot for a mother—who may be an unprincipled adventuress herself, for aught you know?"

"Go on," said Wilton, calmly. "I know you have a good deal more to say, and I am quite prepared to hear it."

"Can you be such a besotted blockhead at this time of life, after having got over the wild-goose period, and not so badly either ; when you have just been offered your first good chance, when a sensible marriage is so important, as to throw every consideration to the dogs for a madness that probably a month or two will cure, and leave you two-thirds of a lifetime to eat your heart out with useless regret ? You know I do not pretend to despise women, or to talk cynical rot about them ; they are generally good, useful creatures, and deucedly pleasant sometimes ; but, God bless my soul, lad ! they are of no real importance in a man's life. It is very essential to marry the right sort of girl, I grant—that is, a well-bred, healthy, good-looking lassie in your own grade of life, you will bring a good connection to back up your children ; but to rush into matrimony—downright legal matrimony—with a creature that scarcely knows who she is herself, because, indeed, you think no other ' she ' in creation so likely to suit you, is a pitiable piece of lunacy. Come ! in the name of common-sense, of self-respect, be a man ! Tell me how you stand with this girl, and let me see if I can't get you out of the scrape."

"Have you quite done?" asked Wilton, leaning back in his chair without the slightest symptom of irritation.

"I have."

"Then hear me, Moncrief! I do not dispute a syllable you say. It is all unanswerable—just what I should say myself to another fellow on the brink of such a leap in the dark. Don't suppose I am blind to the apparent folly I am about to commit. But I'll do it! Nothing can hold me back! I shall not attempt to explain to you the sort of fascination Ella Rivers has had for me from the first moment we met; it would be speaking an unknown tongue, even if I could put it into language. But if her people were all you picture, by Heaven! I do not think I could give her up. Foolish lunatic—besotted as you choose to think me, I have full faith in the woman who will be my wife before five days are over. There! Consider the question 'to be or not to be' settled. Pity my idiotic folly as you will, but do not discard your old *protégé*. I want your advice on one or two points."

"But, Wilton, I must—" began the major.

"Don't," interrupted Wilton. "Remonstrance is sheer loss of time and breath; if you persist, I will leave you to finish your port alone."

Moncrief succumbed, though with an ill grace, and

Wilton proceeded to lay the question of exchange into a regiment already in India, or one about to proceed there, before his ancient mentor, and gradually drew him into better humor, especially as he noted that Wilton's professional ambition was by no means dulled or engulfed by the tide of passion that swept him away in another direction.

"Well, I never thought I should find you looking forward contentedly to a life in India," said the major, after a long and animated talk, anent the *pros* and *cons* of Wilton's views ; "you used to long for a stake in the 'old countrie.'"

"Yes ; but that was because Lord St. George put it into my head. Now, that is at an end."

"Ah ! just so—this infernal marriage ! What do you intend to do with him, eh ? "

"I have not given it a thought—or, rather, scarcely a thought. I will marry first, and decide after. I tell you candidly, Moncrief, when first I made up my mind to risk everything, rather than part with Ella, I had a stupid, cowardly idea of a private marriage ; but I soon gave that up ; it was too deucedly ungentlemanlike ; and then Ella would despise even a shadow of double-dealing ! No ; when we are married, and I have time, I will write to the old viscount, and—"

"By George ! this is too bad," cried the major,

getting up and pacing the room in an agony. " Fortune, and fair prospects, and—and everything flung overboard, for the sake of a white-faced bit of a girl that you would forget in two months if you made the first stand. It's like giving up drink or cigars; the first week is the brunt of the battle ! "

" Don't talk blasphemy," returned Wilton, sternly ; " nor waste time and breath."

" Well, well ! " resumed the rebuked major ; " look here, do not be in too great a hurry to write to the old peer. I met St. George Wilton to-day ; he told me Lord St. George was down at Brandestone, and very shaky ; perhaps you had better not write to him till the honeymoon is over. O Lord ! won't you be ready to cut your throat when you get his answer ! But I trust he will die, and leave you the property in the meantime."

" He will not do that," said Wilton, gravely. But, tell me, what is St. George doing in town ? I hate that fellow instinctively."

" Oh, he was only passing through *en route* to join some ' Lord knows who ' at Cowes, to cruise somewhere in his yacht, and—Where are you going ? "

" Why, you will not take any more wine, and, as I have not seen Ella to-day, I thought I would just run down and bid her good-night. Come with me, old fellow, do ! I'd take it as a real bit of good-fellowship;

she would be so pleased. You may as well submit to the inevitable with a good grace."

"Go with you to see this—ahem!—fascinating little witch? Not to get the step I've been waiting for these seven years."

15

CHAPTER X.

THE extremely sudden and unorthodox character
of Ella's nuptials was a source of irritation, not
to say dismay, to the worthy Mrs. Kershaw. She
took, upon the whole, a desponding and distrustful
view of human nature ; and, instead of meeting Ella's
smiling, blushing account of Colonel Wilton's visit
and her engagement to him, with effusive sympathy,
she had nodded her head and knitted her brows, asked
a dozen questions, and received the replies in ominous
silence ; at last spoke as follows :

"Well, I hope it's all right " (the " hope" in
italics), "but it's curious—very curious. Are you
quite sure he is Colonel Wilton ? "

" Yes."

" How do you know ? "

" Because he was frequently at Brosedale, and
known to Sir Peter Fergusson."

" Ay, to be sure, that's true !   I suppose it's to be
a private marriage.   We must see that it is quite correct, for, high or low, a wife has her rights.   What did
he say about going to church ? "

"Oh ! I scarcely know ; something about my having been three weeks in the parish, and—"

"Did he ?" returned Mrs. Kershaw ; a more satisfied expression stealing over her face. "That looks like business, only I trust and hope he has not a wife already."

"What a fearful suspicion !" replied Ella, shuddering, while she smiled. "He was looked upon as an unmarried man at Brosedale, for I remember that Donald remarked that Miss Saville could find time to amuse him now, because Colonel Wilton condescended to visit him, and that he would be a peer, a nobleman, one day."

"A peer ! a lord ! well, I never ! Of all the queer turns, this is the queerest. Still, I would like to make sure that there is no hitch nowhere. But, bless your heart, no gentleman or nobleman would go to church with a girl unless he was all square."

"I must trust him utterly, or not at all, he said. I do trust him," said Ella, softly, to herself, "even as he trusts me." She was sitting on the hearth-rug, gazing dreamily at a small but bright morsel of fire held together by fire-bricks.

"Trust is a word I never liked," observed Mrs. Kershaw, who was sitting bolt upright in an easy chair. "Ready money, in everything, is my motto ; still, I must say, this gentleman seems straightforward." Mrs.

Kershaw's opinions had become visibly modified since the rank of her fair *protégés* intended had been revealed to her.

" I think he is," said Ella, simply.

" Anyhow, I will speak to him myself to-morrow," continued Mrs. Kershaw, "and let him know you have a friend to look after you as knows the world," she added, emphatically. Silence ensued; for, in truth, Ella was too glad of the cessation of Mrs. Kershaw's wiry voice to break it, when that lady burst out again with a jerk : " You'd best take my parlors—they ought to be thirty shillings a week, but I will give them to you for a guinea."

" But why must I take them ? " asked Ella.

" Because— Why, my patience, Miss Rivers, you are not going to turn stingy, and you going to be a great lady. Why must you take them ? Because it is only decent and proper ; there's scarce room to turn round in a three-cornered cupboard like this place. I'm sure a fine, handsome man like the colonel hasn't room to move here ; and then for the wedding. This day week did you say ? Why, whatever shall we do about wedding clothes ? Still I wouldn't say nothing about putting off ; you'd better strike while the iron is hot ! But *have* you thought of the wedding clothes, Miss Rivers ? "

"No, I do not want any. I have more clothes than I ever had in my life before."

" I declare to goodness you are the strangest young girl—lady I mean—I ever met ; so mean-spirited, in a manner of speaking, in one way, and no more knowing the value of money in another, than a half-saved creature ! Why, you have nothing but blacks and grays."

" And may I not marry in gray ; but if it is right I shall be very pleased to have a pretty new dress and bonnet ; I have quite money enough, you know."

" Well, I must say it is aggravating that we can't have a regular spread, and carriages and favors ; wouldn't that nasty, humbugging, stuck-up-thing, Mrs. Lewis, over the way, that is always insinuating that I haven't laid down new stair-carpeting because I couldn't spare the money—wouldn't she be ready to eat her own head off because she wouldn't be asked to step across ? "

But in spite of Major Moncrief and Mrs. Kershaw, Ralph Wilton had his way, and they were married on the appointed day. The major was so far mollified that he stood by his favorite " boy " on the memorable occasion ; nay, more, with some hesitation he produced a pair of lump gold ear-rings, largely sprinkled with turquoise, as a small and appropriate gift to his friend's bride, when, to the dismay of all present, it was found that the pretty little ears they were destined to adorn had never been pierced.

"It is no matter," said Ella, taking his hand in both hers, "I should rather keep them, just the very things you thought of, than let them be changed! You like me for his sake now ; you may yet like me for myself."

To this the major gravely replied that he did not doubt it, and watched her with observant eyes during the ceremony. The keen old soldier was touched and impressed by the steady composure of her manner, the low, clear music of her firm tones. It seemed to him as if she had considered the value of each vow, and then took it willingly ; he was surprised when the service was concluded, and he again took her hand to find that, although outwardly calm, she was trembling from head to foot.

They returned to Mrs. Kershaw's house, where that excellent housewife had provided a comfortable and appetizing luncheon—the major having the honor of escorting her back. "I can tell you, sir," he used to say in after-years, when recounting the episode, "I felt devilish queer when I handed the landlady into the brougham and took my place beside her. If she had been a buxom widow, or a gushing spinster, I could have stood it better ; but she was such a metallic female! her hair curled up so viciously, and there was such a suspicious, contemptuous twist in her nose, as if she was perpetually smelling a rat, that I was afraid to speak to her. I know I made an ass of myself. I remember saying something about my friend's good luck, thinking to propitiate her, but she nearly snapped my head off, observing that time would show whether either of them was in luck or not."

The luncheon, however, was duly appreciated by the mollified major, Mrs. Kershaw herself, and, we regret to add, the bridegroom, who was in radiant spirits. There was something contagious in his mood —something inspiriting in the joy that rioted in his bright brown eyes—even Mrs. Kershaw lit up under his influence, and for awhile forgot the suspicious character of the human race. But the repast was soon over. Wilton was anxious to catch the tidal train, and Ella went obediently to don her bonnet and travelling-gear.

"Look at this, Moncrief," said Wilton, when they were alone, holding out a miniature in a slightly-faded morocco case ; " it is a picture of Ella's father."

Moncrief scrutinized it with much interest. An exquisitely painted portrait, it represented a dreamy, noble face, dark as a Spaniard, with black-blue eyes, closely resembling his daughter's, a delicately-cut, refined mouth, unshaded by moustache, and a trifle too soft for a man ; the turn of the head, the whole bearing more than conventionally aristocratic, picturesquely grand.

"There is no question about it, Wilton, this man looks every inch a gentleman. Have you any idea who the mother was?"

"Not the most remote. I do not think Ella has an idea herself; she says she had a charming picture of her mother, but it disappeared soon after they came to London, and she has never been able to find it. She has a box full of letters and papers up stairs, and, when we return, I shall look through them and try to trace her father's history, just to satisfy my sister and yourself. Ella will always be the same to me, ancestry or no ancestry."

"By-the-way, where are you going?" said the major.

"Oh! to Normandy—to a little out-of-the-way place within a few miles from A——, called Vigères. There is very good salmon-fishing in the neighborhood, and we shall be quiet."

"When shall you be back?"

"I cannot tell; I suppose I must not take more than six weeks' holiday."

"Well, I would not write to old St. George till you come back."

"I am not sure about that; I—"

"Here is Miss—I mean Mrs. Wilton," interrupted Moncrief.

With sweet, grave simplicity, Ella offered a parting kiss to her husband's friend. Mrs. Kershaw stepped jauntily to open the door. A hearty hand-pressure from Moncrief, whose rugged countenance was sorrowfully sympathetic, and the newly-wedded pair were away.

"Won't you step in, sir, and take another glass of wine?" said Mrs. Kershaw, with startling hospitality, to the uneasy major, who felt in comparative captivity, and by no means equal to the occasion.

" No ; I am much obliged to you," said the major, edging toward the door.

" A little bit of pigeon-pie, or a mouthful of cheese, or a drop of stout to wind up with," persisted Mrs. Kershaw. "You may say what you like, there's nothing picks you up like a drop of stout."

" No, I thank you ; nothing more."

" I hope everything was to the colonel's satisfaction?" resumed Mrs. Kershaw, with an angular smile.

" He would have been hard to please if he had not been satisfied," returned the major, with grovelling servility ; and, taking up his hat, tried, by a flank movement, to get between the enemy and his line of retreat.

" I am sure he is a real gentleman, and knows how to behave as sich. It is a pleasure to deal with liberal, right-minded people, what isn't forever haggling

over sixpences and shillings.   But, between you and
me, sir, though I am none of your soft-spoken, humbugging sort, I never did meet the match of Miss Ella
—Mrs. Wilton, I mean—she is that good and steady,
a wearin' of herself to the bone for any one that wants.
And for all the colonel's a fine man, and a pleasant
man, and an open-handed man, if ever he takes to
worriting or bla'guarding, I would help her through
the divorce-court with the last shilling that ever I've
scraped together rising early and working hard ; you
mind that."

With these emphatic words, Mrs. Kershaw flung
the door suddenly wide open, and the major, bow-
ing, hastily shot into the street, with a rapidity more
creditable to Mrs. Kershaw's eloquence than his own
steadiness under fire.

CHAPTER XI.

OH! the bliss of those early days! The strange sweetness of their new companionship! The weather, too, was propitious—balmy and mild, though spring was yet young, with unutterable freshness and hope in its breath and coloring. The delicious sense of safety from all intruders; the delight of being at home with Ella; of winning her complete confidence. Never before had Wilton tasted the joy of associating with a woman who was neither a toy nor a torment, but a true, though softer, comrade, whose every movement and attitude charmed and satisfied his taste, and whose quick sense of beauty, of character, and of the droll sides of things, gave endless variety to their every-day intercourse.

Theirs was no mere fool's paradise of love and kisses. Sketching and fishing, the days flew by. Wilton had decided that the little inn at Vigères was too noisy and uncomfortable to be endured, and Ella had found lodgings in the house of a small proprietor, who sometimes accommodated lovers of the gentle craft, and, moreover, found favor in the eyes of the landlord and his bright-eyed, high-capped Norman cook and house-keeper, her fluent French and knowledge of foreign housewifery exciting admiration and respect. It was a straggling, gray-stone edifice, just outside the village, with a very untidy yard behind, and a less untidy garden in front, where a sun-dial, all mossed and lichen-covered, was half buried in great, tangled bushes of roses and fuchsias ; on this a large, scantily-furnished *salon* looked out, and beyond the garden on an undulating plain, with the sea and Mont St. Michel in the blue distance, with a dark mass of forest on the uplands to the south—a wide stretch of country, ever changing its aspect, as the broad shadows of the slow or quick-sailing clouds swept over it, or the level rays of the gradually lengthening sunset bathed it with the peculiar yellow, golden spring light, so different from the rich red tinge of autumn. Winding round the base of the abrupt hill on which Vigères, like so many Norman villages, was perched, was a tolerably large stream, renowned in the neighborhood, and, though left to take care of itself, still affording fair sport. It led away through a melancholy wood and some wide, unfenced pasturage, to the neglected grounds of a chateau, with the intendant of which, Wilton, aided by Ella, held many a long talk on farming, politics, and every subject under the sun.

These rambles had an inexpressible charm—a

mingled sense of freedom and occupation. Then the repose of evening, as night closed in ; the amusement of watching Ella at her work or drawing ; to lead her on to unconsciously picturesque reminiscences ; to compare their utterly different impressions and ideas—for Ella was not self-opinionated ; though frank and individual, she was aware her convictions were but the echo of those she had heard all her life, and she listened with the deepest interest to her husband's, even while she did not agree. These pleasant communings were so new to Wilton, so different from all his former experience, that perhaps time has seldom sped on so lightly during a honeymoon. Ella was utterly unconventional, and yet a gentlewoman to the core, transparently candid, and, if such a term can be permitted, gifted with a noble homeliness that made affectation, or assumption, or unreality of any kind, impossible to her. Whether she made a vivid, free translation from some favorite Italian poet at Wilton's request, or took a lesson from him in tying flies, or gave him one in drawing, or dusted their sitting-room, or (as Wilton more than once found her) did some bit of special cooking in the big, brown kitchen, while Manon looked on, with her hands in her apron-pockets, talking volubly, she was always the same—quiet, earnest, doing her very best, with the inexpressible tranquillity of a single purpose. Then the shy tenderness and grace of her rare caresses—the delicate reserve that had always something yet to give, and which not even the terrible ordeal of wedded intimacy could scorch up—these were elements of an inexhaustible charm—at least to a man of Wilton's calibre.

It was evening—the evening of a very bright, clear day. Wilton had started early on a distant expedition, with a son of their host for a guide, and had returned to a late dinner. It had been too long a walk for Ella to undertake, and now she sat beside her husband under the window of their *salon*, in the violet-scented air of an April night, as it grew softly dusk. Wilton was enjoying pleasant rest, after just enough fatigue to make it welcome, and watching, with a lazy, luxurious sense of satisfaction, the movements of Ella's little deft fingers, as she twisted some red ribbon into an effective bow, and pinned it upon an edifice of lace, which Wilton could not quite make out.

"What can that thing be for, Ella? You are not going to wear it?" he asked, at last.

"Wear it? Oh, no! It is for Manon; she begged me to make her a Parisian cap. I advised her to keep to her charming Norman head-dress; but no! Monsieur le Curé's house-keeper has a cap from Paris, and Manon is not to be outdone; so she gave

me the lace, and I contributed the ribbon. Do you
know, this lace is very lovely? Look at it."

"I suppose it is; but I am glad to find you admire
lace; I was afraid you were above dress."

"Indeed I am not; but I always liked—I had
almost said loved—lace. I would prefer lace to
jewels, if the choice were offered me. And then a
hat or a bonnet is a source of joy, if they suit me."

"And we have been here nearly a month—"

"A month yesterday," observed Ella, softly, with a
happy smile.

"Time passes quickly in paradise," said Wilton,
leaning caressingly toward his companion.—"But, I
was going to say, we have been here a month, and you
have never had a chance of shopping. It is a dear
delight to shop, is it not?"

"I do not know," replied Ella, laughing, and turning her work to view it on all sides. "I never had
any money to spend in shops."

"I should like to see you under fire—I mean in
temptation. Suppose we go over to A—— for a day
or two; that is the nearest approach to a dazzling
scene we can manage?"

"As you like; but, dear Ralph"—looking wist-
fully out over the garden—"I love this place, and am
loath to take even a day from the few that remain to
us here. I suppose we must soon leave for London?"

" You would like to stay here always ? "

" No," returned Ella, " certainly not ; stagnation would not suit either of us, though I deeply enjoy this sweet resting-place. It will soon be time to move on."

" We have a fortnight still before us, so we will run over to A—— to-morrow. Our host can lend us his *shandradan*, with that monstrous gray mare, to drive over there. I know you expressed a great wish to sketch some of those picturesque old towers as we came through, and you shall buy some lace if you like. I have had so much fishing that I shall come back with renewed zest after a short break."

" Yes ; I should greatly like to take some sketches in A—— ; but, as to buying lace, do you know we spend a quantity of money here—I am astonished and shocked to think how much ? "

"Then I am afraid I have been a very extravagant fellow, for I do not think I ever spent so little in the same space of time before. But, talking of money reminds me I must write to Lord St. George. I have forgotten all about him—all about every one except you, you little demure sorceress ! "

" Do not forget him, if he is old and a relation."

" Well, I will write to him to-morrow. It is not much matter ; he will never see my face again."

" Because you married me ? "

" This is really a very picturesque place," said
Ella as they strolled through the principal street of
A——, and ascended the plateau, once adorned by a
cathedral, " but, after all, there is more cheerfulness
in English scenery. I miss the gentlemen's seats, the
look of occupation, the sense of life that springs from
individual freedom. Tyranny and want of cultivation
—these are the real 'phantoms of fright.' "

" Yes ; we have never mistaken license for liberty
in England," returned Wilton, with genuine John-
Bullism.

" Thanks to your early training," said Ella, smiling ; " but if for centuries you had never been allowed
to stand or walk without leading-strings, supports,
restraints on the right hand and on the left, and had
then been suddenly set free, with all accustomed stays
wrenched from you, do you think you would not have
stumbled and fallen like your neighbors ? "

" True, O queen ! but why did not our neighbors
begin to train themselves in time ? They are of different stuff ; there lies the key to the puzzle."

" And in the might of circumstance," put in Ella.
" You can never thank Heaven enough for your insu-
lar position ; but there *is* something in race."

" No doubt of it. Look at this man coming
toward us ; you could never mistake him for anything
but a Briton."

16

" No, indeed ! " exclaimed Ella ; " and "—drawing a little near to him—" is it not your cousin, St. George Wilton ? "

" By Jove ! you are right, Ella. What can bring him here ? "

The object of their remark was facing them as the colonel ceased to speak.

"Ralph Wilton—Miss—" St. George stopped himself in his exclamation, and then continued, raising his hat with a soft but meaning smile, " I little thought I should encounter you in this remote region ! "

" Nor I you," returned Wilton, bluntly. " Mrs. Wilton and I have been staying near this, at a place called Vig'res, where there is very tolerable fishing, and drove over this morning to look at this old town. What brings you so far from the haunts of men ? "

" The vagaries of an old woman, if it be not too irreverend to say so," replied St. George, raising his hat again with profound respect as his cousin pronounced the words " Mrs. Wilton." " I have an aged aunt who, for some inscrutable reason, chooses to mortify her flesh and spare her pocket by residing here. I never dreamed I should meet with such a vision of happiness as—Mrs. Wilton and yourself in this fossilized place."

There was just a slight, significant pause before

the name " Mrs. Wilton," which caught her husband's ear, and it sounded to him like a veiled suspicion.

" Where are you staying ? " he asked.

" Oh, at the Hôtel du Nord. My aunt wishes the pleasure of a visit from me, but declines to put me up."

" We are just going to dine at your hotel," said Colonel Wilton, " and will be very happy if you will join us."

St. George accepted his cousin's invitation with his best air of frank cordiality. It was a very pleasant dinner ; nothing could be more agreeable than the accomplished *attaché*. His tone of cousinly courtesy to Ella was perfect ; his air of well-regulated enjoyment positively exhilarating. Wilton never thought he should like his kinsman's society so much. Even Ella warmed to him comparatively, and, though more disposed to listen than to talk, contributed no small share to the brightness of the conversation.

At last it was time to undertake the homeward drive to Vigères, some four or five miles up and down hill. While waiting for the remarkable-looking vehicle in which the journey was to be performed, St. George Wilton found a moment to speak with his cousin alone.

" And it is a real *bona fide* marriage, Ralph ? "

" Real as if the Archbishop of Canterbury had

performed it, with a couple of junior officers to help him."

St. George was silent, and affected to busy himself in preparing a cigar. Not even his trained self-control could enable him to command his voice sufficiently to hide the enormous contempt that such a piece of frantic insanity inspired.

"So very charming a person as Mrs. Wilton," said he at last, blandly, "may well excuse the imprudence of a love-match; but let me ask, merely that I may know how to act, is it an open as well as a *bona fide* marriage? I mean, do you wish it concealed from our friend Lord St. George, because—"

"Certainly not," interrupted Colonel Wilton. "I have not written to inform him of it, for he has left my last letter some months unanswered, and I did not think he cared to hear from me; but, as it is possible he may fancy I intended to make a secret of my marriage, I will write to him to-morrow."

"It is not of much importance," said St. George, checking the dawning of a contemptuous smile. "Whatever view he takes of the subject will be inimical to your interests. Suppose I were to call upon him and explain matters? I start for London to-morrow morning."

"I will not trouble you," said Wilton a little stiffly;

and Ella, appearing at that moment in the door-way, the conversation took a different turn.

"Draw your cloak closer, Ella," said her husband, as they proceeded homeward under the soft silver of a young May moon at the sober pace which was their steed's fastest; "there is a tinge of east in the wind. I began our acquaintance by wrapping you up, and I see I shall always be obliged to make you take care of yourself."

"I take care of myself *now*," she replied, nestling nearer to him. "I did not think your cousin could be so agreeable," she continued.

"Nor I," said Wilton, shortly.

"Yet," resumed Ella, "I can never banish my first impression of him."

"What was it?"

"That he could always keep faith in the letter and break it in the spirit; that he could betray in the most polished manner possible, without ever committing any vulgar error that law or society could fasten upon."

"Upon my soul, you have made a very nice estimate of the only member of your new family with whom you have come in contact. And where, pray, have you found such well-defined ideas of treachery? I did not think there was so much of this world's lore in that pretty little head. How did you learn it?"

"Ah, treachery is a thing I have often known ! The wonder is, as my father used to say, that, where so many powerful temptations surrounded us, poor political outcasts, so few proved false."

"Yet you have not learned to be suspicious, Ella ? "

"Heaven forbid !   No one who is *really* true at heart ever *really* learns to be suspicious."

Wilton fulfilled his intention the following day, and wrote a short, simple account of his marriage to Lord St. George, regretting that he should be a source of disappointment to him, and stating that he, of course, held him quite exonerated from any promise, implied or not, respecting his property.

It was *quite* a relief to him having accomplished this.   He had now cut himself adrift from all chances of social preëminence ; it remained to work up in his profession, and his thoughts naturally turned to India. Great changes, civil and military, were pending there ; his own services had been recognized by men high in office ; already the breath of the outer world had somewhat withered the loveliness of his Arcadia—it was time for him to be up and doing.

"Ella ! come here, darling.   I am afraid we must go back to London and common life next week ; so let us make an expedition to Mont St. Michel to-morrow.   How does the tide serve ? "

Three or four happy days were spent in visiting the strange fortress-prison and Old-World picturesque little town of Granville ; in delicious rambles and abundant sketching. Ella was absolutely excited by the wealth of subjects, all of a new character to her, which offered themselves for her pencil. But Wilton had exhausted his slender capacity for repose, and, having thoroughly enjoyed himself, was once more longing for active life.

The day but one after their return from this brief expedition, a letter reached Wilton from the family solicitor. He had been out smoking, and talking of farming with the landlord ; and Ella remarked, as he took the letter, that he exclaimed, as if to himself, "From old Kenrick! what can he want?" His countenance changed as he read : and then, throwing down the letter, he cried, "I wish to Heaven I had written to him before! He has passed away, doubting me!"

"Who?" asked Ella, trembling with a sudden apprehension of evil.

"Poor old St. George!—the old man of whom I have spoken to you."

"Your marriage has not broken his heart, I trust?"

"No : I am not sure he had a heart to break. But, Ella, you have turned pale, my own darling! Do not torment yourself; the living or dying of every one

belonging to me can never affect my happiness with
you ; you are worth them all to me.   But this letter—
here, read it."   And, passing one arm round her,
Wilton held out the letter for her to peruse.   "You
see," he continued, " Kenrick (he is Lord St. George's
solicitor and the Wiltons' solicitor generally) says he
has died suddenly without a will.   I am his heir-pre-
sumptive and nearest of kin—the only person entitled
to act or to give directions.   We must, therefore,
start for London to-morrow.   I will see Monsieur le
Propriétaire, and settle with him at once."

Ella sighed, and cast one long look out into the
garden, where the bees were humming and the first
roses blooming, and away over the variegated, map-
like country beyond, with its distant, dim blue line of
sea—a farewell look at the scene where she had tasted
for the first time in a somewhat sad existence, the
divine cup of full, fresh delight ; then, holding her
cheek to her husband's kiss, gently disengaged herself
and went away to prepare for turning over a new leaf
in the book of life.

CHAPTER XII.

"THERE is not the slightest use of making any search for a will. I know there is none. Lord St. George made me carefully destroy the last one he had executed only the day before his death. Indeed, he had given me instructions to draw up another so exceedingly inimical to your interests that I determined to be as slow as possible in carrying out his intentions. Now, his death intestate has left everything to you, Colonel Wilton—I beg pardon, my lord."

So spoke Mr. Kenrick—a grave, well-bred, exceedingly professional man—as Wilton sat at the opposite side of his knee-hole table in the well-known office of Kenrick and Cole, Lincoln's Inn Fields, the morning after his arrival in London.

"No; I prefer being Ralph Wilton still. I suppose I need not adopt the title if I do not like? We must remember, Kenrick, that poor St. George's daughter may be still alive, and may have a host of children."

"That is certainly possible, though it is a possi-

bility I had wellnigh forgotten. Forgive me for
saying so, but I heartily wish you had been a little
less impetuous. Six weeks' patience would have seen
you possessed of ample means to support your title,
and free to choose a wife where you liked."

"Ay; but who could foresee the course of events?
I could not have acted a double part with the poor
old man, nor could I have postponed my marriage.
In short, there is no use in discussing the question;
tell me what Lord St. George said when he sent for
you."

"I found him," replied the lawyer, "looking terribly ill, although, as usual, accurately dressed and
quite composed. I had, by his directions, brought
with me the will he had executed a few months ago—
a will bequeathing everything to you, Colonel Wilton.
His first question was, 'Have you heard that my heir
has selected a wife at last?' I replied I had not;
and he went on to say that you had at first concealed
your marriage, but, having met Mr. St. George Wilton,
and thinking concealment no longer necessary, you
had written to him. He showed me your letter, and
said he had a visit from your cousin, who gave him a
true version of the affair, with much more that was
not flattering, and need not be repeated. He then
made me destroy the will in his presence, and gave
me instructions to prepare another, by which he

bequeathed his large property to the Foundling Hospital, adding a grim jest as to the probability of some of his own grandchildren profiting by the bequest. I must say, however, that he seemed principally affected by the apparent attempt to conceal your marriage."

" That was never my intention," said Wilton, much disturbed, while he walked up and down. " But I wish to Heaven I had written to him at once! The fact is, I knew that I had cut myself off from him completely by my marriage, and thought it little mattered when I announced it. Then I forgot to write."

" And most things, probably," said Mr. Kenrick, with a grave and slightly compassionate smile. " The next morning my late client was found by Saunders— his man, who has been so long with him—lying placidly on his bed, but life was quite extinct. He must have been dead some hours."

" I cannot tell you, Kenrick, how confoundly sorry I am to have caused him this annoyance ! "

" His heart had long been in a very weak state," continued the lawyer, scarcely heeding the interruption; " and his death was certainly painless. It remains to discover his daughter's children."

" Or herself," put in Wilton.

" She is dead—I feel sure of that. I perfectly remember my father mentioning to me the terrible species of exultation with which Lord St. George heard that his only child was no more. That must be twenty years ago. I am under the impression that she left no family. If so, I shall be pleased to congratulate you, colonel, on a noble inheritance."

Wilton took another turn to and fro. "I have never been used to wealth or finery," he said. "If I could dispense with the title, I should not care much. Tell me—does nothing hang on to the coronet?"

"Well, I believe the rent of one farm ; barely four hundred a year. But the house in S—— Square belongs to you. It was one of the 'bad' viscount's purchases ; and though the late lord's father paid off the various mortgages with which it was loaded, he never alienated it from the direct line."

"So much the better for me. And now, Kenrick, lose no time in taking proper steps to discover the daughter's children."

"I will, of course ; but I have a strong idea there are none."

"Why?" asked Wilton.

"Because we should have been sure to have heard of them. The father—a needy foreigner, by all accounts—would never have resisted the temptation to dip his fingers into such well-filled pockets as those of Lord St. George ; and the application would have been through us, or referred to us. No, I cannot help thinking Madame or Mrs. de Monteiro left no children."

"And I cannot help thinking she has. When is the funeral to take place?"

"The day after to-morrow. Meantime, had you not better take up your residence in S—— Square? The house is yours, and probably everything in it."

"No, Kenrick; I could not stand the house, nor could Mrs. Wilton, I am sure. I shall remain at the hotel where we now are. After the funeral we must examine the poor old man's letters and papers; we may find some clue to the real heir among them."

Meantime an outline of the story began to be told at the clubs and dinner-tables, now throbbing with the convulsive life of the season.

To the older members of society the name of Wilton had once been familiar, but Ralph had little beyond regimental renown and a high reputation at the Horse Guards. Now, however, that he was supposed to have inherited the estates as well as the title of Lord St. George, relatives and connections gathered round him "thick as leaves that fall in Valambrosa."

Ella was at first bewildered, as well as surprised, at the numerous cards and polite inquiries for Lord and Lady St. George, until Wilton unfolded the whole history for her enlightenment, and expended some bad language on the annoyance of being thus saddled with a title he could not support. Still he was sufficiently alive to the necessity of his position to insist on his wife's supplying herself with proper and fashionable mourning at the most select milliner's he could find out. The result delighted him and appalled Ella. The garments were certainly becoming, but never in her simple life had she seen so much money paid for clothes.

The operation of examining the papers and letters of one lately alert and ready to defend the privacy of his inner life is full of mournfulness. Even when the deceased has been neither well known nor loved, there is deep pathos in the silent appeal of death. All the secrets of the now empty " prison-house " lie bare and at the mercy of a successor, who may be the last to whom the released tenant would have exposed them. Although Ralph Wilton was far from being a senti- mentalist, he felt this keenly when, assisted by Mr. Kenrick, he proceeded to examine the late viscount's escritoire, and various caskets, cabinets, and jewel- cases, in hopes of finding some trace of his possible successor. There lay, in profusion, the graceful trinkets bestowed with lavish hand on his wife and child, exquisite enamels, carved onyx clasps and brooches, costly fans, old-fashioned *bijouterie*—all the beautiful artistic trifles which accumulate in an ancient and wealthy family. The more important jewels were of course kept at the bank, but quantities of valuable nothings were scattered about the rooms—miniatures of fair women and lovely children, and one beautiful face in every stage of development, from an infant peeping out from its rich surrounding of lace and satin to a stately, gracious demoiselle in court dress. These portraits were all in rooms and cabinets the most distant, dust-covered, and evidently rarely opened. All bore somewhere about the frame the initials E. L. A., sometimes plain, sometimes entwined in a monogram.

"'These are all portraits of Miss St. George," said the lawyer, in the law tone they both unconsciously adopted. "You can scarcely wonder that such a marriage should almost have driven her father mad. He hardly thought royalty good enough for her."

"What, in Heaven's name, made her throw herself away on a foreigner?" exclaimed Wilton. "How could she be so mad?"

"Hum!" said Mr. Kenrick, dryly; "imprudent marriages are always incomprehensible, except to those that commit them."

Wilton looked up for a moment, with a flash of indignation in his quick, brown eyes, which, passing rapidly away, gave place to a good-humored smile.

"You are right," said he; "no outsiders can quite judge the force of our unreasoning reasons. You had better dine with us to-day, and let me present you to Mrs. Wilton."

" I imagine she expects you to present me to Lady St. George."

" You are mistaken. She is utterly indifferent to titles—more indifferent than I am ; but you will dine with us ? "

" I shall be most happy."

But they sought in vain ; no trace existed of the viscount's erring daughter after the period of her disgraceful marriage. Of private correspondence very little remained, and it was decided to advertise for the information they wanted.

" Let us have some talk with Saunders," suggested Wilton ; " he was so much with Lord St. George that he may be able to give us some clue to what we want."

The serious-looking valet was therefore summoned, and the lawyer shortly explained to him the state of affairs.

" I believe there was an application of some kind made to my lord respecting his daughter," said he, slowly and reflectively ; " but it was a long time back —nearly three years ago."

" Tell us what you know about it," said Wilton.

" It was in the summer time, just before we left for Scotland that year, and my lord was not very well, when one morning the hall-porter called me and said there was a foreign gentleman wanted to see my lord

about a picture. I knew he expected one or two he
had bought in Italy, a few weeks before, to be sent
after him—the only thing he seemed to care about
lately was art ; so I went and spoke to the gentleman
—for, though he was a queer-looking customer, he did
not seem a common fellow. He spoke a sort of broken French, and said he was Italian (I can speak
French, but not Italian,) and added that he had called
to see Lord St. George about a picture. So, as he
seemed quite fit to speak to my lord, I went and
told him. He says, 'Show the fellow up.' I did so,
and left them together. I waited outside, in case my
lord should want me, and presently I heard them
thundering at each other in Italian—not that my lord
spoke very loud, but there was that in his voice as
would make any man jump. Presently he rang very
sharp ; I went in and found him half-raised in his
chair, holding on by the sides as if he would dig his
fingers into them, as white as marble, and his eyes
blazing fire. There was some torn paper lying at his
feet, and a picture in an open case on the floor at a
little distance. The foreign chap," continued the valet,
warming into naturalness, "was standing looking at
him with a dark frown on his face—the sort of murderous scowl those Italians can put on—and I went
close up between them, lest he might draw a knife.
'Turn this scoundrel out !' says my lord ; 'and mark

17

him, Saunders; if you ever find him loitering about
the place, hand him over to the police!' With that
the foreigner gave an odd sort of smile, and said a
few words in Italian, hissing them through his teeth.
My lord's face changed as he listened, but he waved
his hand toward the door; and the other, with a deep,
low bow, walked out. My lord had a sort of fainting-
fit, and I was a good deal taken up with him, but I
kept the picture, thinking the Italian might come back
for it; but he did not. I think it is a miniature of
my lord's daughter, for it is very like all the other
portraits."

"But the pieces of torn paper," asked the lawyer,
quickly—"did you not by accident see if anything
was written on them, and what?"

"Well, sir, as I was picking them up, I did see
that the writing was English, though a foreign-looking
hand; but all I could make out was, 'Your only
daughter's only child so soon to be an orphan.' Then
my lord fainted away; and when I looked for them
again the stupid girl had swept them up. I can bring
you the picture, if you wish."

"By all means," said Colonel Wilton; and the
man left the room.—"I wish to Heaven," he continued, "he had kept the letter instead of the picture!
We have portraits enough of the unhappy girl; the
letter might have put us on the track of the heir or

heiress. Do you think this Italian was the husband?"

"Di Monteiro was, I believe, a Spaniard; but Saunders might mistake Spanish for Italian ; and then the statement in the letter, ' the only child of his daughter so soon to be an orphan '—that might be by the death of either father or mother. But, no ; it is quite twenty years since the mother died."

Here the return of Saunders interrupted the lawyer's conjectures.

"This is the picture," he said, unfolding it from some silver-paper in which it was carefully wrapped. The case of dark-purple leather had a foreign look ; on opening it a lovely face, most exquisitely painted, appeared. It was unmistakably the same as that so frequently represented in the deserted chambers of the mansion ; but changed and saddened and spiritualized in expression.

"This is very beautiful," said Wilton, looking long and earnestly upon it. "Though evidently the same face as the others, there is something familiar to me in it which the others have not. I can fancy a man daring a good deal for such a woman as this ! However, it brings us no clue. We must consult some of these wonderful detective fellows and try what can be done by extensive advertising. You must now feel satisfied that my poor cousin has left an heir or heiress."

"Heiress, I trust," replied Kenrick. "A foreign Bohemian, with the recklessness of poverty, and perhaps Communist principles, would be a terrible representative of the house of Wilton; a woman would be less dangerous."

"Nevertheless, quite as objectionable, unless caught very young; and, according to your account she must be past twenty. However, we can do no more to-day; and, by Jove, it is nearly six o'clock! Mrs. Wilton was to have met me in Kensington Gardens on her return from a visit at Notting Hill. I shall be scarcely in time to meet her. We dine at seven-thirty, and shall have the pleasure of seeing you?"

"I shall be most happy; I am very anxious to have the honor of making Mrs. Wilton's acquaintance."

"Well, then, will you be so good as to take charge of this picture? I see you have your inevitable black bag, and it is rather large for my pocket. Pray, bring it with you this evening. My wife is a true artist, and will be charmed with it."

In these days of pressing occupation, it was a rich treat to Ella and Wilton to have an hour or two uninterruptedly together. A visit to some of the art exhibitions, to the opera, or to a good play, was sufficient to brighten whole days of comparative loneliness. Ella was eminently reasonable. She never

tormented her husband to know why he was not in
time, or indulged in querulousness if he was compelled
to break an engagement. She knew he regretted it
as much as she did, and was satisfied.

On this occasion she had waited patiently, sitting
under a tree near the Bayswater Gate for nearly a
quarter of an hour before the sight of her husband's soldierly distinguished figure, approaching rapidly, made
her heart leap for joy.

" I am late ! but I could not help it. And what
have you been doing? How is the benevolent Mrs.
Kershaw ? "

" Very well, indeed ; but a little indignant because
we did not take her 'drawing-rooms,' which were
vacant when we came to town, instead of going to be
cheated, as she says, ' up *and* down ' at a hotel."

" And what did you say ? " asked Wilton, drawing
his wife's hand through his arm as they strolled
toward town.

" Oh ! I told her you had so much to do, that
Melina Villas was too far away. But, O, dearest
Ralph, I really think dear old Diego must have called
there while we were in Normandy. Mrs. Kershaw
was out, unfortunately, but the servant described a
' tall, black-looking gentleman, who had very little
English.' He asked first for Mrs. Kershaw, and then
for me. Now, no one could ask for me but Diego."

"And, my darling, what is Diego like? is he a gentleman?" asked Wilton, rather doubtfully.

"Yes, certainly, a gentleman; but not like you. He wears a velvet coat—it is charming when it is new; but he has not always money, then it gets shabby; I have seen it broken at the elbows; and he has a felt hat, oh! such a beautiful hat at first—but—I fear he sleeps in it sometimes, for it gets much bent. But, when Diego has his purse full, and new clothes, he is lovely! I have sketched him when they were new, and mended them when they were old. He is handsome, like a Salvator-Rosa brigand. You would think he could kill; and he is really as gentle and simple as a child. You are much more fierce yourself, Ralph "—looking up lovingly into his eyes, with very little fear in her own. "How I should like to see him again!" she continued; "if we meet, you must ask him to dinner."

Wilton laughed heartily.

"If we do meet, I shall; but he will be a curious guest. Let us have our distinguished cousin, St. George, to meet him."

"Would it annoy you, Ralph, to have poor Diego to dinner?"

"No, love; but don't ask him to live with us, I could not stand that."

"Nor I," said Ella, quietly.

Talking pleasantly, they enjoyed the sunshine of a lovely afternoon, till Wilton, looking at his watch, declared they would be late for dinner, and hailed a hansom.

It was very gratifying to Wilton to observe the effect produced by Ella on the sedate Mr. Kenrick, who was an old-young man. Her unconsciousness of self gave her a high-bred composure; her perfect freedom from provincialism—the result of having acquired English almost as a foreign tongue—an air of refinement, and her natural, simple readiness to listen, only caring to speak when she really had something to say, gave a charm to her conversation which greatly impressed the cool, hard-headed man of business. However blind love may be, no man, unless below the average of intelligence, is so hoodwinked as not to see when other men think he has a good excuse for his imprudence or not.

The gentlemen did not sit long after Ella had left them, and, on joining her, Mr. Kenrick observed, " I have brought the picture, Colonel Wilton, as it is your pleasure to be so called."

And he handed a small parcel to Wilton, who, opening it, said, " Look at this, Ella."

She was cutting the leaves of a book which Wilton had bought that morning, and, looking up quickly exclaimed, " Ah! how good of you! you have found my picture for me.   Where did you find it?"

" Your picture! what do you mean?" he askèd.

" The picture of my mother, which was lost."

"You are under some mistake.   I do not think you ever saw this before."

" I have seen it all my life; it is my mother's picture."

" Your mother's!" exclaimed Wilton and the lawyer together; "impossible."

" Yet it is so.   If you raise the frame here, at the side, you can take it out of the case, and you will find her name at the back—Elizabeth Louisa Adelaide di Monteiro—mine is formed from her initials of her Christian name."

The lawyer and Wilton eagerly obeyed, and found the inscription as she had described.

"This is very extraordinary!" exclaimed Wilton.

" It appears, then," said Mr. Kenrick, " that, by a rare accident, you have married your own cousin, and Lord St. George's heiress.   The title and estates are united."

" How?   What does he mean?" asked Ella.

" Tell me, Ella, was Monteiro your father's name?"

" Yes, one of them.   His mother was a wealthy Spanish lady, his father an Englishman.   He was partly brought up in Spain, by his mother's people, in

her name ; he was early an orphan, and, I imagine,
very extravagant. Afterward, when immersed in politics, he found it more useful to use his father's name of
Rivers. He was peculiarly averse to mention my
mother. I never knew her family name. Her picture
was always a sacred thing. My father, who might have
been a great artist, painted it himself. Now, tell me,
what do your questions mean?"

Whereupon Wilton, holding her hand in his, told
her, as shortly as he could, the strange story of her
mother's marriage and disappearance; of the displeasure of her grandfather at his (Wilton's) disregard
of his wishes in the choice of a wife ; of the consequent
destruction of the will, and the difficulty in which he
and Mr. Kenrick found themselves as regarded the
next-of-kin ; with a running accompaniment from the
lawyer touching the nature, extent, and peculiarities
of the property inherited by the obscure little heroine
of Wilton's railway adventure.

"All this mine, which ought to have been yours,"
said Ella, when they were at last silent ; "or, rather,
yours through me—I do not seem able to understand
or take it in."

She pressed her hand to her brow.

" Dearest, you believed in me, and loved me, when
I was desolate and poor, and utterly insignificant ;
now I am thankful that I can bring you wealth ; but

oh ! I gave you most when I gave you my whole heart ! "

Extract of a letter to VISCOUNT ST. GEORGE, *from* MAJOR MONCRIEF —*th Rifles.*

" I shall certainly be with you on the 12th, if nothing unforeseen occurs. I feel exceedingly curious to see you in your new home, and to thank Lady St. George personally for the plenary absolution she has so kindly extended to me. I confess myself guilty of the cold-blooded worldliness you lay to my charge, while I acknowledge that few men have had a better excuse for a piece of extraordinary imprudence. If we were mere bundles of high-toned emotions, sympathies, and aspirations, marriages on your system might answer ; but, being as we are, much more animal than spiritual, more self-seeking than sympathetic, is it wise to act on the impulse of a temporary brain or blood fever, which puts a certain set of fancies and desires in violent action for a time, only to be overtaken and swept away by the everlasting flow of every-day wants, ambitions, and motives, which always run their course, however excitement may blind us ? But I am growing too profound for an old soldier ; the upshot of the argument is that I stand to my opinion in a general sense ; your extraordinary luck in no way touches it. But I most warmly rejoice in your good fortune ; and, though I greatly regret your quitting the old regiment, I am not surprised that your new position necessitates the step. Yours is no common story ; and I little thought, when I was 'taken prophetic' the day you 'interviewed' poor old St. George, that so fair a lot would be the ending of 'Ralph Wilton's Weird.'

" Always your sincere friend,

" A. MONCRIEF."

THE END.